TOO GOOD TO BE TRUE

THE SIREN ISLAND SERIES, BOOK FIVE

TRICIA O'MALLEY

LOVEWRITE PUBLISHING

TOO GOOD TO BE TRUE

The Siren Island Series

Book Five

Cover Design:

Damonza Book Covers

Editor:

Elayne Morgan

"Nothing is ever 'too good to be true.' If it came into your life, it means you have earned it. Simply enjoy it." – Akin Olokun

PROLOGUE

*M*irra drifted with the current, enjoying the pull of the water as it flowed over her fin, stretching her arms in front of her to revel in the weightlessness of being surrounded by the sea. Here, she was home. It was on land where she was constantly awkward, running into corners, and blushing when anyone paid her too much attention. Her twin sister, Jolie, had confidence in spades while Mirra preferred to take a quieter backseat to her antics. It was only when she returned to the sea that Mirra felt like she could truly be herself, and there she found the confidence she wished for on the shore.

Now, diving deep, she pulled herself from her meditation and let herself tune into the flow and rhythm of the ocean surrounding her. It wasn't difficult to do – not for a mermaid, at least – and she was able to read the energy of the reefs around her to see if there was anything in distress. Periodically, Mirra would spend an entire evening searching the reefs for turtles caught in fishing line, or cleaning up trash stuck on the corals. She considered it an underwater gardening of sorts, and liked to keep the reefs around her island as tidy as could be.

When the distress call came, Mirra's head went up. Closing her eyes, she sent out her power, like a sonar wave of magick, to find out where she was needed. The call went up again and tears spiked Mirra's eyes as she surged forward, faster than any fish, and barreled toward where her friends were in trouble. Heart pounding in her chest, she came to an abrupt stop when she stumbled on the source of the call.

Dolphins were caught in a large-scale commercial fishing net. An entire pod of them, mothers and babies alike, all screamed to her for help.

Desperate, Mirra surfaced briefly, taking a quick scan of the situation. The boat was large, a whaler-type ship, and she knew they hadn't caught the dolphins by accident. Large cranes creaked as they pulled the nets in, and her friends panicked, shrieking frantically in the dark water.

Diving below the surface, Mirra circled the net, sending a blast of calming magick to the dolphins and instructing them to huddle together in the middle so as not to get their fins caught in the net. From the sheath at her side Mirra drew a silver knife, impossibly sharp and blessed with magick from Poseidon himself. She focused, and got to work.

Her blade sliced neatly through the thick cable, but when it snapped, the cord whipped around her middle, ensnaring her in a hole in the net.

"Go!" Mirra urged, gasping for breath as she wrestled with the cable biting into the flesh at her waist. "Get out of here. I'll be fine. Save yourselves!"

Mirra blasted the dolphins with her urgency and they streamed through the opening she'd created, fleeing from captivity and certain death. But once outside the net, they swam deep below her – far away from any chance of being captured again, but refusing to leave Mirra's side. Mirra could hear the dolphins sounding the alarm, trumpeting for help from her brethren.

She gasped as the cable tightened, threatening to cut off her breath, and reeled her toward the boat. Dots sparked her vision, and Mirra knew she was only moments away from death.

"Help…" Mirra whispered, struggling desperately while trying to cut the cable once more. "Please…"

CHAPTER 1

A sharp bark made Silas put his binoculars down and turn to look at his small dog – a bastardized mix of Jack Russell terrier, yellow Lab, and a dash of island mutt – who had propped his paws on the railing of the deck.

"What's that, Splash? Do you see dolphins?"

Silas Somerborne was a man of the sea. Moving as easily across the deck as on land, he swayed naturally with the rocking of the boat as he crossed to see why Splash had sounded the alarm.

It was his fifth year working in Marine Park and Coastal Enforcement for Siren Island. Prior to that he had bounced around the Caribbean, working various jobs on everything from luxurious yachts to enforcement. His time on Siren Island had been his longest stint, and one that he'd found suited him. Silas played by the rules, those of nature and of island law. Together, those two tenets guided his daily path.

Content with his job in enforcement and protection of

little Siren Island, Silas could, for the first time, say he felt comfortable staying in one spot. He'd even adopted an island dog – or he supposed it was more accurate to say Splash had adopted him. He'd shown up on Silas's dock one morning, and when he'd taken pity on the young pup and invited him on board, their future together had been sealed. Splash had taken to being a boat dog like a fish to water, and had turned out to be all the companionship Silas needed.

Or wanted, for that matter.

He'd left home at fourteen, taking his chances that the streets would be kinder to him than his pathetic excuse for a father had been. He'd hitched his way down to Florida where he'd found a job loading container ships for a company that didn't ask too many questions. He'd kept his head down, worked hard, and saved his money. The minute he'd turned eighteen, Silas had disembarked in sunny Antigua and had been bouncing around the Caribbean ever since. He'd made some friends along the way, and had even enjoyed the warm embrace of many a willing woman – but the thought of having one nattering in his ear all day? No, thank you. He and Splash were just fine on their own. Why did anyone need a woman when there were good books and tasty rum to be enjoyed?

Silas patiently scanned the horizon, knowing that Splash rarely barked for no reason. Something was afoot, and Splash had sounded the warning about whatever it was that had caught his attention. When a school of flying fish glinted in the air, Silas glanced down at Splash.

"Is it those guys? I know you like the fish, but you usually don't make a fuss when you spot them."

lowed in the sunlight, a sleek curved number that looked wicked and deadly.

With no better options, Silas grabbed her knife and brought it to the cable that wound its way several times round her waist, lancing into her skin. She writhed in pain. "Shh, just don't move. Please."

His eyebrows rose as the knife sliced neatly through the cable. When it finally snapped free, the woman let out a little gasp, and shuddered as she drew in a deep breath.

"I've got you. Just stay with me. I'll get you back to the boat."

Silas glanced up to where the fishermen stood watching. Seeing that the woman was cut free, they now gunned their engines to make an escape. He held tight to the woman as the waves created by the boat crashed over them forcefully, almost capsizing the woman from her position on the life ring. If he lost her now, she'd sink straight to the bottom – of that he was certain. Holding his breath, Silas sank under the surface of the water to push the float above him. When he couldn't hold his breath any longer, he surfaced by her side and steadied her.

"It's gonna be okay, hun. I promise."

His boat had drifted some distance away, and with the other Marine Park Enforcement boat in full pursuit of the fleeing fishermen, Silas had quite a swim on his hands. He cursed long and low, then focused on the crisis at hand.

"You'll be just fine. I've got you. You're safe now," Silas promised the woman even as he saw the blood seeping from the bare skin at her waist. When something brushed his leg, Silas closed his eyes and prayed it wasn't a shark, tempted closer by the scent of blood in the water.

Splash bounded across the deck and put his paws up on the other railing. A jaunty red bandana was tied at his neck, and he tilted his head as he looked out over the water.

"So, not the fish then. Hmm."

Silas brought the binoculars back to his eyes and took his time moving his gaze across the horizon. Finally the smallest of blips caught his eye.

"Okay, I see it. There's a boat way out there. Farther out than it should be, if it's one of our recreational boats. Let me check the logs to see if anyone's radioed in."

Silas returned to the steering wheel. He accessed the maritime tracking app to see what boats were in the water, as well as the day's logs for arrivals and departures. He did notice a boat on the tracker, but his suspicions were raised when no vessel information was listed. Silas picked up his radio to call it in.

"Vessel has no documentation and has not requested docking approval," his radio squawked.

"Well, well, well," Silas murmured. "Copy that. Going to check it out."

After relaying the coordinates and requesting backup from the larger Marine Enforcement vessel docked at the harbor, Silas set course for the boat.

It wasn't uncommon that a recreational boat or a local fishing boat, sometimes undocumented, suffered with engine trouble or other mechanical problems. But, judging from both the distance on his dash panel and what he could see through the binoculars, this boat was much larger than a local fisherman's. It wasn't out of the realm of possibility that he was dealing with something much more dangerous

– like drug runners. Silas checked his weapons to make sure his pistol was loaded, as well as the larger carbine he sincerely hoped he wouldn't have to use today.

"Splash, into the galley."

Splash dutifully followed orders and jumped down the slanted ladder to the galley below. Silas didn't know what he would do if someone harmed his dog, and he certainly wasn't interested in finding out today. Once he was sure Splash was safe, Silas closed the door to below deck and increased his speed to approach the mysterious boat.

As he brought the binoculars back to his eyes, Silas swore. He was gaining on the vessel and he could see men racing across the stern, and a wide-open space in the hull. This meant they might be fishing for large illegal game like sharks or dolphins. There was nothing that made his blood boil more than illegal fishing expeditions that killed gentle mammals like whales or attacked beautiful sharks for the shark-fin trade. He could only hope he'd made it before any of the sea life had been caught.

Radioing the information and the coordinates, Silas sounded the alarm to the fishing vessel. "This is the Siren Island Marine Park Enforcement. Stop immediately and turn your engines off. Back up is on the way. You cannot escape. I repeat, cut your engines. Backup is on the way. This is the Siren Island Marine Park Enforcement."

His adrenaline kicked up, heart pounding in his chest, while his focus narrowed to the net in the water. He couldn't see any fins thrashing about, so maybe he'd arrived in time. His gaze bounced back to the deck where men were shouting – not at him, but down at the water.

Trailing his eyes back, Silas's heart skipped a focused on what they were panicking about.

There, caught in the net, was a woman. A nal that. She struggled with the cable wrapped a waist – and even as she fought, the cable was dr under.

Silas swore. Turning to see that the larg Enforcement vessel had arrived, he threw his neutral. Grabbing his knife and a life ring, Sila ladder over the side and dove into the water, k focus on the woman in the net. There was no te she had come to be in such a predicament, and knew these fishermen had no qualms about whales and dolphins, he hoped they'd balk at human.

With quick strokes, Silas reached the net an where the woman had slipped under the water. past the saltwater that stung his eyes, he f woman's arm and pulled her to him. Silas k feeling the drag of the net, and worked to roll th on top of his life ring.

Once he'd steadied her and made sure her hea of water, Silas grabbed for his knife and begar steadily at the cable wrapped around her waist. once more – his knife barely made a dent. The s was too thick to cut.

His eyes flew to the woman's face when she for him. "Use this…"

The woman coughed and gestured with the kn hand, which was unlike any he'd seen before. I

When a dolphin surfaced at his side, Silas almost shouted in relief. "Hey, guy. I hope none of your family was in that net."

To his shock, an entire pod surfaced around them. The dolphin nudged him again, and Silas suddenly realized what they were doing. A rush of awe went through him. "Oh my god, you're helping me back to the boat. Thank you!"

Silas hooked an arm around the dorsal fin of the dolphin nearest to him and allowed the dolphin to pull him through the water at a speed far faster than he could have ever achieved on his own. In a matter of moments, the dolphins had escorted them back to the boat — and now Silas was faced with a dilemma of getting the woman on the loading deck by himself.

"Any chance you can stay with her while I climb up?" Silas asked the dolphins, knowing he was being foolish. The dolphins couldn't actually understand what he was saying. But remarkably, they somehow did seem to understand what he wanted — they circled the life ring and helped to keep the woman afloat.

Silas didn't want to think too hard about what was happening. He hoisted himself up the ladder, then leaned over the side and reached his hands out. He was surprised once again when the dolphins pushed the woman forward. When she was close enough, he scooped her up and pulled her on board, laying her flat on the deck.

Turning, Silas eyed the pod. "Thank you," he said, offering them a quick salute before turning to tend to the woman in front of him. He'd lived on the sea long enough to know there wasn't always an explanation for the way animals behaved, and in this instance, he could only be grateful for their assistance.

Silas checked the woman's breathing, then got up and raced across the deck to grab the first-aid kit. When he returned, he dropped to his knees beside her and winced as he studied the soft flesh at her waist where the steel cable had sliced into her. Her wounds looked fierce, and he feared for her life.

"My name is Silas," he began, going through the first responder drill. "I'm here to help. Can I touch you?"

The woman opened eyes the color of the sea at dawn and nodded to him.

"I'm going to bandage your waist and then we're going to get you to the doctor. Do you understand?"

"I do." The words, but a whisper, sent a shiver over his skin. Working quickly, Silas did the best he could to bandage her and stop the bleeding. He had to lift her up to wind the bandages all the way around her waist, and Silas couldn't help but think how good she felt in his arms. Now wasn't exactly the time to be having amorous thoughts, but it was almost impossible not to see how beautiful the curves of her body were.

Steering his thoughts away from such matters, Silas finished bandaging her. "I'm going to lift you up and carry you out of the sun. I'll need to drive to get you back to shore, and I want to make sure you're safe."

"Thank you."

"Of course. Just save your energy. We'll talk more about how this happened later."

Silas neatly picked the woman up, again marveling at how she felt in his arms, and brought her into the shade, then wrapped her in several blankets and gave her some water. When he was finally certain she was as stable as could be, he dropped to his knees by her side once more and leveled a look at her.

"Do you like dogs?"

A faint smile creased her pretty face. "I love dogs."

"Splash is going to keep you company while I get us home."

Silas opened the hatch and whistled for Splash, who bounded up the ladder and onto the deck. The dog's head whipped up as if catching a scent, and he immediately raced to the woman's side. Jumping up, Splash curled next to her without waiting for Silas's command. The woman's arm reached out to wrap around the dog's furry body. "Good dog."

With a million questions unanswered, Silas set his course for shore. The most important one being, how had the woman ended up in a net this far from shore, and why hadn't she drowned when she was held underwater for so long?

CHAPTER 2

*I*t was him.

He was the one she'd been waiting for. As sure as she knew that the moon mothered the oceans, Mirra knew this man was meant for her.

It was funny, really, this sense of knowing. There was no explanation for it, other than a subtle little *click* that had resounded in her heart when she'd slitted her eyes open to see who was pulling her from the water. Like the final puzzle piece finding its home, this man held part of her soul as she did his.

A muscular man, with intricate tattoos wrapping both tanned arms, he radiated confidence and the type of edge that came with authority. Authority over whom, Mirra couldn't be certain, but this was a man who didn't look to others for answers. Sunglasses shaded his eyes, and his dark hair was cropped close to his head. She wondered if he smiled often.

Mirra stroked the dog that nuzzled into her side. She had a natural affinity with animals, and now they both

"Did…were the dolphins safe?" Mirra asked, and she saw a hint of surprise cross Silas's face.

"You were worried about the dolphins?"

"Of course."

"It looks like they made it out. And they were apparently quite grateful because they helped me get back to the boat with you on the float. I've never seen anything like it."

"They've got good souls."

"They do at that, Ms. Mirra. Shall I hold onto your knife for now? It's…well, I have some questions. But the doctor is here."

"Yes, hold it for me. I'll come get it."

"You don't know where I live."

"I'll find you." Mirra smiled, then her attention was distracted by a paramedic kneeling by her side. In moments, they'd assessed her wounds and loaded her onto a stretcher.

Mirra closed her eyes and let her mind drift, knowing that Silas would keep his word and contact her family. For now, she needed to focus on saving her energy so she could heal her wounds. Her mind floated, taking her back many years to her first oracle reading – a rite of passage for every mermaid when they came of age – and something she'd never fully shared with anyone.

He'll rescue you. But then you must rescue him. His heart is guarded and he knows little of love. Only you can teach him what that means, and he must learn it before your souls can bond.

He *had* rescued her. Quite literally. The moments of terror came back to her, then fell away as she realized that

sought comfort from each other. She could already re:
that Splash was a happy dog and well cared for, whi
raised her estimation of the man who had rescued her.

Mirra winced as she adjusted herself on the bench, an
took shallow breaths against the pain that lanced her sides.

"Your name?" Mirra asked, but realized her voice
was but a whisper. Splash looked up and issued a sof
bark, causing the man to turn and look at her. "Your
name?"

"What's that?" The man immediately came to her side.

"Your name?" Mirra repeated.

"Silas. We're almost to the dock. I have medical
personnel waiting."

"Call the Laughing Mermaid. It's a guesthouse. My
family."

"On it."

Silas. Mirra rolled the name around in her head, liking
the sound of it. Silas and Mirra. Together they would be
happy – of this she was sure.

Mirra stayed quiet, concentrating on funneling her
healing powers into her wounds, and watched while Silas
docked the boat and radioed for someone to contact her
family. Knowing she was in good hands, Mirra closed her
eyes again.

"Are you still with us?" Silas asked.

Mirra opened her eyes to look up at him. "Yes. Just
conserving my energy."

"What's your name?"

"Mirra."

"Mirra… I don't know how you landed in the position
you did, but I'm glad I got there in time."

the pain and fear had been necessary on the path to finding him.

"Mirra!"

Mirra blinked her eyes open. She must have dozed off – she was now in a hospital room – and Jolie and Irma were trying to push inside the room. A nurse stalled them at the door and spoke a few murmured words before the two raced forward.

Irma, a woman more sea goddess than human, grasped Mirra's hand and placed her other hand on Mirra's brow. With the age-old touch of a mother, radiating love, she smoothed her daughter's forehead. Mirra could feel it pulse gently over her, and she responded with the same, their energies colliding in a healing force to ease her pain.

"How did this happen?" Jolie asked, worry etched on her beautiful face.

"It was a bit silly, really. I should have moved faster. I was freeing the dolphins from a net and I wasn't paying enough attention to how I cut the cable, so when it snapped, it caught me up in it. Steel cables and bare skin… not a good match." Mirra smiled ruefully.

"Oh, Mirra. You could've drowned or been snapped in half! You're lucky you don't have organ damage or internal bleeding. They think you could have scars," Jolie exclaimed.

"So be it, then. The dolphins are free and I'm safe."

Jolie's eyes were drenched in sadness.

"We can help with her scars too, Jolie, as you know." Irma squeezed Mirra's hand. The faint beep of the heart monitor was the only sound in the room for a bit as they absorbed the news of Mirra's injuries.

"Are you in much pain?" Jolie finally asked.

"I am. But I'll be okay. I promise. I have other things on my mind."

"How can you have other things on your mind when you nearly *died*? I would have the whole island in here bringing me gifts by now." Jolie tossed her mane of dark curls over her shoulder.

"Because…I met him. My soul mate."

"Oh, Mirra. You did?" Jolie brought a hand to her heart.

"I did. He's the one who saved me."

Irma arched a brow. "Well, then I believe we owe this young man a thanks, don't we? Perhaps a visit?"

"Oh, I'm definitely going to visit him. Maybe not all of us at once, though. It could be overwhelming for him. He seemed to be a solitary sort."

"Handsome?" Jolie got down to what were, in her mind, the important details.

"Handsome. Muscular. Heroic. He dove into the water to save me with not a thought for his own safety."

The women all sighed.

"And he has a dog – a really happy and well cared for dog."

The women all smiled at that.

"His name is Silas," Mirra continued, squeezing Irma's hand once more before removing it from her grasp so she could adjust herself in the bed. "And he has my knife, so I have to go see him."

Jolie's mouth dropped open. "You let him see the knife?" It wasn't generally allowed for humans to handle mermaid-charmed weapons, and there could be backlash from the mermaid world.

"I had no choice. It was the only thing that could cut the cable to get me loose."

"Then you will face no repercussions, I can promise you that," Irma reassured her.

"He definitely seemed interested in it."

"Who wouldn't be? It's nearly impossible to pretend it isn't magicked."

"Well, he didn't seem too bothered by the dolphins helping us back to the boat, so maybe he's open-minded to mermaids?" Mirra said hopefully.

"He's going to have to be if he's your person. Otherwise, we'll bash him over the head with it until he comes around," Jolie declared.

"There ya go." Mirra smiled. "Just beat your man into submission. I'm sure that will go over well."

"Let's start with thanking the man and inviting him to a nice dinner," Irma suggested.

"I get the sense he's going to be standoffish. I've never seen him on island, and it's pretty clear he works for the marine park. I feel like we would have seen him by now unless he's not sociable."

"I wonder why that is." Jolie eased herself down to sit on the edge of the bed.

"I don't know. I was too busy bleeding all over his boat to ask questions." Mirra quirked a smile at her sister.

"I seriously can't stand to think of you bleeding out. It makes me nauseous." Jolie held her palms to her stomach.

"It made me nauseous too," Mirra laughed.

"How long will you be in here for? Did they say?" Irma asked.

"I think they want to keep me a while for observation, but hopefully I can come home tonight." Mirra yawned.

"We'll go to the store and the pharmacy to make sure we have everything you need. Are you craving anything special I can make for you?" Irma asked.

"Mmm, I feel like maybe it's best to keep it light. I can't imagine being bloated would feel good with these wounds," Mirra admitted, shifting uncomfortably in the bed.

"Hmm…what about, like, smoothies or gelato? Italian ice?" Jolie tilted her head at Mirra in question.

"Yes, perfect. I'm sorry to scare you guys."

"It was terrifying getting that call. We had no idea how badly you were hurt. The man who called couldn't tell us your condition."

"I was scared too. But I'm okay now." Mirra yawned again.

"Rest. We'll be back to bring you home as soon as the doctor says you can go."

"I love you both," Mirra whispered before exhaustion claimed her.

"Oh, well, that's not necessary," Silas said. Awkwardly, he patted Jolie's back while she trembled in his arms. "I did what anyone would've done."

"No, that's not quite true." Irma pursed her lips as she studied him with a gaze that felt like she saw straight to his soul. Gently disengaging from Jolie, Silas patted her arm until she composed herself. "Not every man would have abandoned his vessel in open water – unanchored, mind you – and rescued my daughter from a fishing net. It was foolhardy and incredibly courageous. And for that, I am forever in your debt."

"It was what any man would do," Silas insisted, scrubbing a hand over his face. "Yes, it was foolish to jump in the water after her. But I'm a strong swimmer and I knew I had backup coming from the other Marine Enforcement boat. One way or the other, I was going to make it back to my boat. I would have to be a cold-hearted person to stand by and watch your daughter drown."

"Please, will you let us thank you?" Irma asked. "We'd love to have you over for dinner this week after Mirra has recovered."

Silas deflected the question. "How is she?"

Jolie, the sister, spoke up. "She's exhausted and in a lot of pain. More than she's telling us. But we'll work on her. We're good at taking care of our own."

Silas studied her, now seeing the resemblance between the two sisters, even though their coloring was different. Both had sweetly curved lips that made a man want to have a taste, bedroom eyes, and long hair that tumbled past their shoulders. Hell of a gene pool, this family, Silas

CHAPTER 3

*L*eaning against the wall in the waiting room of the hospital, Silas looked up to see two women – each just as gorgeous as the other, though one was easily a couple decades older – scanning the area. The older one's eyes landed on Silas and, with a small nod of recognition, she walked directly to him. Genetics didn't lie, so this had to be Mirra's family. He imagined the three of them together were enough to make any room they walked into go silent. Even now, the other people in the waiting room had stopped their fussing to watch the two women hurry over to him.

"Silas?" the older woman inquired.

"Yes, that's me. I'm assuming you're Mirra's family?"

"You are correct. I'm Irma, Mirra's mother, and this is her twin sister, Jolie." Irma gestured to the woman standing next to her. Silas had a moment to be surprised that they were twins – they were like moonlight and sunlight – before he was engulfed in an enthusiastic hug.

thought, as his eyes tracked back to Irma. He was hard-pressed to say if he'd pick the daughter over the mother; the mother packed just as much of a punch as the daughters did. It wasn't just their looks either – it was something in the way the air vibrated around them. Never had he met women so calmly in possession of their own personal power before.

"I'd like to see her before I go," he said. *Why?* he wondered silently to himself. There was no reason for him to stay when Mirra was clearly attended to. Yet he couldn't bring himself to leave without seeing her.

"Of course. I'll clear it for you when we leave," Irma replied. "She's tired, but I'm sure she'd like to thank you herself."

"I don't need thanks. I'd just like to see that she's well."

Irma measured him again with those all-seeing eyes, and Silas, for the first time since he was a young boy, felt like squirming in his shoes.

"Trust doesn't come easily to you, does it?" Irma murmured.

"I always like to assess the situation with my own eyes," Silas said. He'd been right about the woman seeing too much, and his back went up.

"Well, assess away, then. You'll come for dinner, yes? Please say yes. It's the least we can do. Mirra is the best of us and you saved her." Jolie grabbed his hand and drew his eyes back to her.

"I'll see about it. I've got a busy week on the boat."

"We'll be in touch. Go to her. She'll be pleased to see

you." With that, as if she could sense that their praise was putting him on edge, Irma left.

Silas watched their departure, and when a nurse crossed to him, he shook his head as if to clear his thoughts. "Sir? You're cleared to see one of the patients. She's in room 103. Just down the hall and to the left."

"Thank you."

Silas pushed through the swinging double doors and went down a short hallway to the hospital ward. It was a small hospital with a few air-conditioned wings built around an open-air courtyard. There were only eight rooms in this wing, and he quickly found which one held Mirra. At the door, he saw a nurse checking Mirra's bandages, so he stepped back, out of sight, and waited for her to finish and leave the room.

"Poor thing's exhausted. You're welcome to sit with her a while." The nurse smiled up at him. "I'm sure she'll like the company, whether she knows it or not."

"Thank you, I'll do that." Silas had dropped Splash at home before he'd come to the hospital, and his boss had ordered him to take the rest of the day off. Aside from writing up his report, he didn't have much to do.

Easing himself quietly into the visitor's chair, Silas studied the woman in the bed before him. If he'd been a poetic man, he would have said she looked like a star plucked from the inky depths of a velvet night sky.

She had the same lush mouth as her sister, and dark lashes fanned the curve of her cheek. Her hair – a shade between blond and silver – tumbled about her shoulders, and for some reason Silas itched to wind his hands into it. In fact, he wanted his hands all over her. Never before had he seen or held a woman more perfectly fashioned for a man's hands than this one. She was all soft womanly curves, voluptuous in a way that showed both strength and sensuality, and if he hadn't been so focused on saving her life out there in the water, he might have embarrassed himself by fawning all over her. Now that she was safe, he couldn't help but flash back to the image of her naked body.

Strong and soft, all in one – just the kind of a woman that could make a man lose his mind.

"Silas."

Silas jerked his mind back from where his thoughts had tried to take him and immediately stood. "Mirra." He nodded at her and clasped his hands in front of him respectfully. "How are you feeling?"

"I'm in pain," she admitted, wincing as she shifted in the bed.

Immediately, Silas reached out to help her, putting his hands on her arms to raise her into a more comfortable position. As soon as she was settled, Silas dropped his hands and lightly rubbed his thumbs against his palms. Touching her had felt like touching a live wire, and Silas wasn't sure if he'd be able to let go.

"Should I get the nurse?" He glanced to the door.

"No, it's fine. She just gave me something. I don't like to take too much medication. It makes my head foggy."

"But if it helps with the pain…"

Mirra smiled gently at him. "It's okay to feel pain, Silas. If I numb it totally, I could hurt myself more by moving in a way that disrupts my healing."

Strength, Silas reminded himself. This woman was strong in both body and mind.

"That's a smart attitude to have. I, uh, met your mother and sister. They wanted you to rest, so I won't take much of your time. I just wanted to make sure you were okay."

"I'm well as can be, thanks to you. I owe you a great debt." Mirra's blue eyes held his. "And I don't say that lightly."

"It's what anyone would have done," Silas said again. "What was I supposed to do – just sit there and watch you drown?"

"The men on that fishing boat were going to."

"Well, they might have. They did stop the net from pulling in, though."

"But none of them tried to save me. They were more concerned about their own lives and getting caught than about saving me. So, no, not any man would have done what you did."

"I'm just glad I got there in time. Splash has good eyes."

"Your dog?"

"Yes. Splash sounded the alarm. Otherwise I might have missed it."

"Then I also owe Splash a great debt."

"Listen…I'm uncomfortable with this whole 'owing' concept." Silas rocked back on his heels. "People shouldn't do the right thing just because they think it'll earn them a reward. It's not like a ledger sheet or something. You don't owe me anything; your family doesn't owe me anything. What kind of person would I be if I expected rewards?"

"I hardly think offering you a meal would be considered a reward by any means." Mirra's laugh tinkled out, like a wind chime ringing softly in the breeze, and the sound warmed Silas to his core.

"I just mean it isn't necessary. Knowing you're safe and well is all the thanks I need."

Mirra sat in silence for a moment, looking into his eyes, and Silas got the same feeling he'd had when Irma had studied him. It was like she was reading his soul – seeing too much – and conflicting emotions warred inside him. Part of him wanted to go to her, to wrap his arms around her and always keep her safe, but the other part wanted to run far, far away. This was a woman who would strip all his carefully constructed defenses bare.

"I'm well, Silas. Thank you for checking."

"I should go now. You look exhausted."

"I am." Mirra gave her wind chime laugh again. "I'll not lie about that. But will you sit with me until I fall asleep?"

It was such a gentle request, and one that Silas respected. She didn't try to cover up her pain and wasn't shy about asking for someone's company when she wanted it. There was strength there, again – not being reluctant to ask for what she needed.

"Of course."

Silas drew his chair closer and sat, clearing his throat, unsure if he should ask any of the questions that were racing around his head. Like, how did she get so far out to sea? Where did that knife come from? Why was she carrying a knife and not wearing any clothing?

But his thoughts stuttered to a standstill when Mirra

reached out and clasped his hand. Warmth radiated up his palm, and it felt like all of his nerve endings stood on end. This woman, whoever she was, was a threat to his very carefully constructed existence.

And yet he stayed there, holding her hand, long after she slipped deeply into sleep.

CHAPTER 4

"*S*ilas has declined our dinner invitation. He insists there is no reason to reward him for what any honorable man would do," Irma said, days later. She stood barefoot at the stove, her hair loose down her back and a jumble of bracelets jangling at her wrists. The three of them were in the kitchen at the Laughing Mermaid, the guesthouse they owned and operated together.

"Stubborn, isn't he?" Jolie mused. She was teaching her new dog, Snowy, to shake a paw, but the puppy was far more interested in the piece of cheese she was holding than the command she was trying to teach him. Mirra laughed as Snowy launched himself at Jolie, overwhelmed with excitement.

"Seems that way. Or not used to people going out of their way to thank him," Mirra said.

"You'll take him dinner, Mirra." Irma was already packaging up food and putting the containers in a tidy little basket along with a bottle of wine.

"Of course." Mirra smiled. "He can run, but he can't hide."

"Try not to scare him off," Jolie advised.

"Oh, this from the sister who all but threw herself on Ted? Please. I'm far more subtle than you are," Mirra scoffed.

"I most certainly did not…" Jolie trailed off and then shrugged. "Okay, fine. I was a bit forward with Ted."

"Let me feel him out a bit. I sense he's very guarded, and I want to find out where that comes from. He's not going to open up to me in one night, I know that. I have to play the long game."

"Just keep showing up and bothering him until you've ingratiated your way into his life?" Jolie asked.

"Something like that."

"Report back after. Are you sure you're okay to go? I worry about your wounds," Irma said.

"They're much better thanks to your salves." Irma and Jolie had mixed up some seaweed-based salves and added a dose of magick to them to help Mirra's wounds heal. They had made a tremendous difference, and even though Mirra occasionally winced in pain if she twisted too fast, she was feeling much better. Her mind had been consumed with thoughts of Silas ever since she'd met him, and she wasn't sure she could bear to be away from him for a moment longer. She just *had* to know more about this man who was most certainly meant for her.

"Let me take the basket to the truck for you." Jolie jumped up and grabbed the basket before Mirra could protest. Snowy followed closely at her heels.

"Be patient with him, Mirra. I sense he needs a gentle

touch." Irma wrapped her arms around Mirra's shoulders and softly kissed her cheek.

"I will. You know how softhearted I am. I just can't stop thinking about him, and I know he won't come to me. I'll have to lead this dance."

With that, Mirra left the Laughing Mermaid. She took her time driving to the small bungalow that Silas owned. It hadn't taken much effort to track him down, as the island's "coconut telegraph" was easy to tap into when she wanted information. The sun was just dipping to the horizon as she pulled up, and a light breeze toyed with her hair. Mirra had kept her outfit casual – denim cut-off shorts and a fuchsia tank top made of breezy linen – and had braided her hair back from her head to tumble down her shoulders. As was often the case, she'd forgotten shoes, and now padded barefoot to the gate at Silas's house.

"Knock, knock," Mirra called, spying Silas kicked back in a hammock strung between two palm trees. Splash jumped up at her arrival and bounded over to the gate, putting his paws on the door and grinning up at her. "Hey buddy, good to see you."

"You shouldn't be on your feet." Silas's voice was stern, and when he reached the gate, his eyes narrowed at the basket she carried. "Let alone carrying things. Foolish."

Mirra just smiled up at him. Silas sighed and reached over the gate to take the basket from her. Unlatching the lock, he pushed the door open and gestured for Mirra to enter. Splash immediately pressed his side into her legs, looking up at her to beg for pets.

"I'll pet you when I sit down, buddy. I don't want to bend over."

"If you can't bend over, you shouldn't be out of bed," Silas lectured, his tone gruff as he stood there holding the basket.

"It's better. See?" Mirra lifted the loose linen of her tank top to show her wounds. The scars had formed pink ridges across her abdomen, but Mirra knew in time they'd heal. Silas crouched to examine her midriff, and a shiver raced through her at his nearness. On the breeze she caught a hint of soap and rum. He must have showered after work and now was having a happy hour drink while he read his book. Not a bad life, Mirra mused, as she took in her surroundings.

The garden was nice, but it needed more plants, as far as she was concerned. It was...utilitarian at best, she thought. There were the two palm trees that Silas had strung his hammock to, another in the corner of the yard, and a small table with two chairs. The house was a simple bungalow style painted white, with brown shutters thrown open to the breeze, and an orange clay tile roof. If Mirra had her way, she'd string up fairy lights through the garden and add some potted plants, maybe a hibiscus bush, and put a larger table in the garden for friends to stop by. Perhaps some tiki torches to line the fence, she mused.

"That's remarkable. You've healed quickly." Silas straightened and met her eyes. She was shocked to realize she hadn't registered his eye color earlier. They were a cool grey, like the misting of a spring rain over the water. The color popped in his tanned face, and Mirra found herself swaying gently forward as if pulled to him by some invisible thread.

"My mother worked her magick. She creates a special salve with seaweed and other nutrients from the ocean. It's good for sunburns and such as well."

When Silas just nodded without saying anything else, Mirra tilted her head up at him. "You declined our invitation for dinner."

"It wasn't necessary. A simple thank-you is enough."

"But I'm afraid that's not enough for *us*. My mother, as you'll come to know, is a force of nature," Mirra said with a laugh. "When you didn't come for dinner, she insisted that dinner be brought to you. Have you eaten yet?"

"No," Silas admitted, however reluctantly.

"Perfect. Shall we sit outside?"

"We?"

"Oh, I'm happy to leave it here for you, if you prefer not to have company. But I did bring enough for two…" Mirra trailed off, knowing she was backing him into a corner.

"Right. Okay, at the table here then?"

"It's a beautiful night. I think that would be nice."

Silas turned abruptly and stomped over to the table, and Mirra bit back a grin. He certainly wasn't one to hide his feelings – at least not his annoyance. He stopped at his table and looked down before muttering under his breath and disappearing inside.

Mirra looked down at Splash, who studied the basket hopefully. "Don't worry, I brought something for you too."

Humming, Mirra unpacked the basket and laid out the various food containers, as well as the bottle of wine. She smiled when Silas returned with plates, utensils, and two mismatched glasses. He plopped a small lantern in the middle of the table and lit the wick so that a tiny flame danced light across the table. When Mirra pointed at the wine bottle, he paused and glanced dubiously down at the glasses he'd brought out.

"Those glasses are just fine, Silas," Mirra said.

"Are you sure? I think I have a wineglass or two buried somewhere."

"Not much of a wine drinker, are you?" she asked, amused.

"Here and there. I enjoy rum, primarily."

"Ah, as most sailors do." Mirra smiled when he started to sit and then stopped, turned, and pulled her chair out for her. So the man had manners.

"Except I don't fall into the drunken sailor stereotype. I like to sip my rum. I don't usually have more than one glass a night."

"Moderation is important," Mirra agreed, nodding when he held the wine bottle up to her glass.

"It's more about control, I think. I like to be aware of my surroundings."

Mirra let that bounce around inside her head a bit as she opened the containers of food. She wondered what type of life he led that he needed to be on guard at all times.

"That's certainly smart. Is that because of your job?" she finally asked.

"That's part of it." Silas sighed when Mirra stayed silent and just looked at him. "If you have nobody else to look out for you, it's important to stay alert."

Sensing his discomfort, Mirra only nodded. "I hope you like lasagna. I was in a comfort-food kind of mood. There's lasagna, a spring-greens salad, garlic bread, and a nice tiramisu for dessert. Will that suit you?"

"I'll eat anything." Silas frowned when Mirra looked at him. "I mean, this looks good. Far nicer than what I'd typically make for myself."

"What do you typically make for dinner?"

"I'm easy. I usually throw something on the grill or open a can of beans. Less mess."

"You can't mean you eat the beans cold from the can?" Mirra laughed.

"Sure, why not? They're tasty." Silas flashed a smile at her and Mirra's heart flipped in her chest. This was the first time she'd seen him smile, and his entire face changed from controlled harsh edges to warmth. She decided right then and there that she would try to make him smile as much as she could tonight.

"I'll admit, that's a delicacy I haven't tried yet." Mirra laughed again and spooned salad and lasagna onto his plate. Opening up the foil packet that held the bread, she offered it to him.

"Listen, I'm not fancy. Sometimes easy is best. It may not be high cuisine, but it suits me. Some nights I'll grab takeout from a few of the local spots too."

"Have you tried the new grill place by the water? It's fabulous."

"I was going to the other night, but the line was too long."

"Maybe we could go sometime." Mirra's suggestion was met with silence. Deciding to move on quickly, she kept talking. "It's usually my sister, Jolie, and my mother most nights. My mom loves to cook, and she taught us well. We're always in the kitchen making big meals or concocting desserts for the guests. I'd guess you'd say we're feeders by nature. We like to take care of people and dote on them. Hence this meal."

"Ah, it's making more sense now," Silas said, taking a bite of his lasagna.

"You can run, but you can't hide," Mirra said, and was rewarded with another one of Silas's heart-melting smiles. "Once my mom decides you're part of our flock, you can't shake us."

"You have to know that I don't need this, right? It makes me..." Silas shrugged his shoulders as he stabbed some greens with his fork. "Itchy, I guess. I don't do things because I think people will owe me favors or anything like that."

"Hasn't anyone ever thanked you for something before? Or brought you gifts?" Mirra joked. But when Silas's eyes shuttered, she realized she'd hit on a nerve. "I suppose you're used to managing on your own."

"Yep. Me and Splash, that is. It's not a bad life," Silas said, his cool grey eyes meeting hers steadily across the table. This was not a man who invited pity, Mirra realized, nor would he respond well to it.

"Certainly not. It seems to me you have a nice thing going on here. Pretty sunset views." She gestured to where the sun had dropped below the horizon and the remaining light shone a brilliant pink against the clouds. "A great dog. A hammock in the breeze. A job you...well, I shouldn't make assumptions. Do you like your job? How did you get into it?"

"Into being a sailor? Running away, mostly," Silas said, and then frowned, glancing at the wineglass in his hand. He put it down without taking another drink, and Mirra wondered if he felt he'd said too much. "I enjoy seeing what's over the next horizon, and I like being near water. It was a natural fit."

"How long have you lived here?"

"Several years now."

"I'm surprised we haven't met yet. The island's not that big."

"I keep to myself for the most part. Occasionally I'll go play some dominoes with a few of the old-timers down the road. I'm not one for bars and clubs and all that."

"No, I'm not either," Mirra admitted.

"A pretty girl like you? I'd have thought you'd be out every night."

"Is that right?" Mirra warmed at his compliment. "It's not for me. I do love music and dancing, but I'm happier dancing by a bonfire on the beach than at a club. Less of a crowd and you can hear the music better. Plus, it's fun to dance under the night sky."

Silas was staring at her like he'd lost his train of thought. "That's...sorry, I was just getting a visual of you dancing on the beach. I'm surprised every red-blooded man in the area hasn't raced across the sand to dance with you."

"I'm happy to dance alone." Mirra shrugged. "As for loud bars and clubs...they're just not my thing. I like to be in nature, or in the water, or creating."

"What do you create?"

"Oh, I dabble in all sorts of things." Mirra leaned back, taking a sip of the vibrant red wine Irma had supplied. "I'll make jewelry, clothes, wall-hangings or art for the rooms. Sometimes I go to the clay studio and make pots for plants. That kind of thing. I like to garden, and I feel that's creative as well. Really just anything that strikes my fancy. I like to bring beauty into the world."

"I bet you put cushions on things," Silas said.

Mirra laughed again. "What's wrong with cushions?"

"They clutter the space up. Why put cushions on the bed if you just toss them off again each night?"

"They add warmth and they're comfortable to lean against if you read in bed?" Mirra smiled. She'd already decided she needed to bring him something to warm his place up. Looking around, she decided she would bring him one of her pots with a plant in it. It would be a gift he had to tend to, and she wondered if he would care for it the same way he cared for Splash. The dog clearly adored Silas, and it was obvious the feeling was mutual. "But to each their own, I suppose. Oh! I brought something for Splash as well, because he was also a hero."

"You did?" This time the smile bloomed wide and stayed there. Interesting, Mirra thought. The man refused accolades for himself but was happy to accept a gift on behalf of his dog.

"Yes, he's a noble beast and must be commended as such." Mirra reached into the basket and pulled out a small package, then handed it to Silas. She smiled when he bent over and let Splash sniff it before he carefully opened the bag.

"Let's see what we have here. Look at this, Splash. A nice hunk of rope for you to chew on – your favorite! Oh, and here's a nice bone for you. And…what is this?" Silas held up a knit badge that had the word "hero" emblazoned across it.

"It's a pin to put on his bandana. So everyone knows he's a hero," Mirra explained.

"Would you look at that? You've got your own badge now, boy," Silas exclaimed and dutifully pinned the badge to Splash's bandana. "You look very dignified and proper. Go on now, enjoy your bone. You earned it."

Splash delicately accepted the bone from Silas and wandered to a corner of the garden to enjoy his bounty.

"He seems happy."

"He is. Thank you, that was very nice of you."

"It's interesting that you're willing to accept gifts for your dog, but not for yourself."

"Let me show you what I think is interesting." Silas got up and went back inside. When he returned to the table and set Mirra's knife in front of her, her breath caught. "Care to tell me where you got this?"

CHAPTER 5

"My knife!" Mirra beamed up at him and reached for it. Silas sat down across from her, his face unreadable in the light from the candle.

"It's…quite a knife, Mirra. Where did you get this?"

"It's a gift from the Cave of Souls."

"Is that so? I think you're going to have to explain a little bit more. I've never seen the likes of this blade, and I've seen a lot of blades. And I'm confused, too. I tried it out," Silas muttered.

"Did you? On what?"

"On a steel cable similar to the one the fishermen were using. The one that my own knife couldn't cut through."

"Ah. And did you find it to your liking?" Mirra inquired, already knowing the answer.

"It didn't work. For all its beautiful design and intricate craftsmanship, I could barely cut a piece of bread with the thing. So I have questions." Silas leveled a look at her.

"Interesting." Mirra shrugged. "Perhaps you dulled it when you cut me from the net?"

"Perhaps. It doesn't look all that dull to me." A look of doubt crossed Silas's face. "Though I suppose I did have to cut hard to get through the cable. I guess that could have dulled the edge."

"Thank you for returning it to me. It's special."

"What's the Cave of Souls? Is that a store on island I haven't heard of?"

Mirra laughed, and thought about how to answer. She wasn't ready to fully reveal to him who she was; even though the oracle had foretold his arrival in her life, trust still took time to build. However, it was against her nature to expressly lie to anyone.

"Have you heard the myths of Siren Island?"

"I've heard a few of them. The main one about Nalachi, the one behind the mermaid statue down south. That one?"

"Yes, that's one of them. What did you think of that myth?"

"I think it's sad. Maybe if she had been honest with him to begin with, they would have had more time together."

"Really?" Mirra was surprised by the response. "You don't think it's natural for a mermaid to want to hide what she is? Out of self-preservation?"

"Why? She's more powerful than humans."

"Humans still hunt and capture them."

"But if she'd told Nalachi he wouldn't have been so desperate to find her. They could have just arranged times of the month to meet. It would have been safer for all involved. If she really loved him, she could have been honest with him."

"Yes, but they had some other issues. He held her against her will to force her to reveal herself. Is that a good way to gain her trust?" Mirra argued. She nodded when Silas held up the bottle of wine to pour her another glass.

"Maybe not. But it seems like an avoidable tragedy."

"Maybe. Maybe not. Fate has a way of directing the tide whether we like it or not."

"I'm guessing this Cave of Souls of yours has something to do with the same myth?"

"It's the extended version of the myth, you could say. Not many people hear about what happens after Nalachi dies."

"I'd like to hear." Silas leaned back, a faintly surprised look crossing his face as he glanced down at his empty plate.

"Seconds?" Mirra asked.

"I'm good, thanks. But did I hear you mention tiramisu?"

"Ah, the man has a sweet tooth," Mirra said with a laugh, and dug the small cooler from the basket. Serving them both, she settled back in silence for a moment while they both dug into the decadent dessert. A brief look of bliss crossed Silas's face. Not so immune to pleasures then, she thought.

"This is excellent."

"A step up from a can of beans?" Mirra teased.

"A thousand steps up," he agreed, gesturing in the air with his spoon. "So, the Cave of Souls?"

"Right. So, our young Irmine was heartbroken at the loss of Nalachi. She took his soul and put it into a pearl which she wore around her neck. From then on, when the night seas got rough or large storms blew in, Irmine did her best to warn sailors away from the treacherous rocks. She took it as her duty. When she wasn't around or able to help and a sailor was lost to the elements, she'd collect their souls too. She kept them in pearls in the Cave of Souls. It was a way to ensure the sailors' souls remained safe and protected in the afterlife."

"Is that right? So she collected souls and imprisoned them in a cave. That sounds like the beginning of a scary movie."

Mirra glanced up to protest and found him grinning at her. He was teasing her, she realized, and felt relief flood through her.

"Or one could view it as a comforting thought. Instead of lost souls stealing across the waves each night, they've been given a safe home to live."

"Is that heaven then? What about the concept of rein-carnation? Can a soul move on if it is stuck in a cave?"

"When the soul is ready to move on, you can find the pearl in the water."

"Ah – it leaves its shell of protection and moves on."

"That's right." Mirra smiled at him. Silas crossed his arms over his chest, his tattoos dancing in the candle-light, and Mirra could just imagine herself sitting here with him each night, talking about books and other topics while the breeze played in the palm leaves above them.

"And this is where your knife is from? The cave is real?"

"Of course it is. It's just tricky to find."

"I know most of the topography of this island. I'm

certain I would've known about this cave of pearls if it existed somewhere here."

"Cave of Souls. And I didn't say it was on island."

"Ah, one of the outer islands, then. Interesting. There's loads of little ones around," Silas mused. "I haven't explored all of them yet."

Mirra decided to distract him from trying to track down the cave. "You know what else they say about souls?"

"What's that?"

"That when someone saves another person's life, they own that person's soul now."

Silas looked positively horrified at her words, his mouth dropping open in protest. "No. I emphatically disagree." Candlelight glinted in his eyes, and Mirra was surprised to feel a ripple of anger cross the table.

"Why does that make you angry?"

"Because nobody can own someone else's soul. That's just silly."

"You have mine," Mirra pressed.

"No, I do not. I helped you once. That doesn't mean I'm some, like, soul overlord now who can rule your life." Silas ran a hand over his short-cropped hair. "That's just… that's insane."

"But don't you see? You're the pearl. You protect my soul now. It's yours because without you I would be no more."

"Listen, I was actually enjoying our dinner and all, but this has gotten a little out of hand for me. I appreciate you bringing me food, and you are very welcome for saving your life. I'm glad I was able to help you in your time of need. But that's it. No more. This stops now, do you hear me? Your soul is your own. I don't need any more thanks. You can protect yourself and your own life and all that. Aside from the craziness you just spouted, you strike me as a levelheaded woman who can make good decisions for herself. I rescind my protection. You've got your life under control."

"Do I?" Mirra laughed. Standing up, she began to pack up the rest of the food, knowing it was time to pull back. It was clear that even the hypothetical thought of having responsibility for another being's soul was more than enough to send Silas running. She had her work cut out for her, she realized.

She slid her knife into the basket, happy to have it back. It was still as sharp as could be, but it would only work when she was around to charge it with power. Otherwise, the blade would remain dull and bring harm to none. It was better that way, else mermaid knives could become vicious tools in the wrong hands.

Silas stood and helped her pack the basket. "I mean, aside from the fact you were swimming naked that far offshore with a knife in your hand – which, speaking of... why were you doing that?"

"I'm a free-diver," Mirra said, which technically wasn't a lie. "Periodically I like to go for long-distance swims and check the reefs, see if any turtles are in trouble, that kind of thing. I could hear the dolphins screaming for help in the water and went to investigate."

"Oh, Mirra." Silas shook his head. "Do you have any idea how dangerous it was to confront those fishermen on your own? They have guns, and they have no problem

shooting people – even Marine Enforcement or govern-
ment officials. These are people who only care about prof-
its. You could have been killed."

"I wasn't really aware of what I was swimming into
until I was close. And once I saw the pod panicking in the
net, I couldn't help but try to free them. There were two
babies in there. Do you know what would have happened
to them?"

"They'd be killed or sold to those shitty hotels that
offer 'swimming with the dolphins.'"

"Yes, exactly. And that's no life for a dolphin. They're
meant to be with their pod, out free in the ocean. Do you
know there are instances of dolphins committing suicide in
captivity? They just stop swimming. They don't come up
for air anymore. That's how unhappy they are."

"I'm certainly not disagreeing with your stance on
saving the dolphins. I think the fishermen who do this
should be held in captivity the rest of their lives and see
how they like it. But I can't help but point out, *again,* just
how dangerous the situation was. You could've died."
Silas reached out and almost touched her arm before
catching himself and dropping his hand. "You have to be
more careful. It's not safe to be that far from land. Next
time I catch you that far out in the water, I'll have to fine
you."

"You can't fine me for swimming in the ocean." Mirra
laughed. Though he had roundly refused the responsibility
of protecting her soul, the man was still trying to protect
her in his own way.

"I'll figure something out. I'm sure there's a loophole
somewhere," Silas grumbled as he hooked the basket on

his arm. Seeing that they were up, Splash raced across the yard and stopped at Mirra's feet.

"There's a handsome boy, isn't there?" Mirra put a hand on the table to steady herself and crouched so she could pet Splash. "You're looking very fancy with your badge. Now everyone will respect you for the hero you are."

Splash seemed to agree, tossing his head back and forth before he took up the hunk of knotted rope she'd brought for him and raced back to his corner of the yard.

"There'll be no living with him now. His ego will be through the roof," Silas sighed, causing Mirra to throw her head back and laugh again. As aloof as he pretended to be, he had a dry wit that pleased her. And he clearly had a soft spot for his dog.

"Well, do your best to keep him humble. Thank you for not kicking me out even though I know me bringing you dinner made you uncomfortable. It was nice chatting with you and getting to know you better. I look forward to doing this again soon," Mirra said, leaning against the hood of her truck as he loaded the basket into the backseat.

"It was a delicious dinner. My compliments to the chef, and please tell Irma she is absolved of her debt, or whatever it is."

"I'll relay the message." Mirra noted that he'd made no move to take her up on her suggestion that they meet again.

"Well, then good night," Silas said, stepping through the gate and closing it after him. And that was that, Mirra mused. Already she was shaping up her plan to put a chink in his carefully crafted armor.

"Sweet dreams, Silas. Bring Splash by sometime to play with Jolie's dog, Snowy." She got no response to her words, so she just smiled and gave a little wave before she got in her truck.

Mirra sang the whole way home.

CHAPTER 6

*S*ilas woke before sunrise, as was his habit, and took a moment to calm his racing heart. His dreams had taken him right back to a place he'd spent most of his life trying to forget, the images flashing through his mind like vignettes playing out in a stop-action film.

There was the time he'd been five years old and sent home from school because he'd peed his pants and didn't have a change of clothes. His father, furious about having to take precious hours off work, had backhanded him as soon as they'd gotten home. Silas had raced to the corner and curled into a ball, while his father had ducked his head into the refrigerator and pulled out a beer, taunting Silas the whole time.

"What a loser. Only babies pee their pants. Is that what you are? When are you going to be a real man?"

Silas had tried to explain that the older boys had bullied him and blocked the bathroom during recess. They'd wanted this to happen.

"Bullies? Boy, you'd better be stronger than them. Fight back next time or sit in your wet pants all day. This is your problem to solve."

Fast forward to a year later when he'd gotten into another scrap on the playground and ripped his jeans.

"Boy, I don't have money for new pants. You'll have to live in those."

Silas had learned to stitch his clothes carefully after that, and he'd focused on learning how to be a better fighter, twisting and dodging from blows so his clothes remained largely undamaged.

By the time he'd hit high school, Silas had learned to be on guard at all times – both at home and in school – and when the opportunity had arisen for him to take off, he'd never looked back.

It annoyed him that these dreams still surfaced. He rolled over and wrapped an arm around Splash, who had his head on a pillow next to Silas. The dog turned and burrowed into his side, the warmth of his presence comforting him. He was a long way from the scared boy who had fought his way to freedom, but some of the past still remained.

His thoughts bounced to Mirra.

She was so beautiful that his hands ached to reach for her, but for Silas, she was off limits. She reminded him of one of those crystal fairy globes that hung in the window, designed to catch the light and explode into a rainbow of colors. Both delicate and strong. But Silas feared that if he were to touch her, she'd shatter.

She'd laughed when he'd told her he sometimes ate beans from the can. Of course, she'd had no idea that this habit came from living in poverty and not always having electricity to cook. Not to mention it was a cheap way to get sustenance. The first few years he'd worked the docks, he'd scraped together every penny he could to afford to crash on the couch in one of his co-workers' miniscule trailer homes.

He'd been lucky, though. His co-worker, Michael, hadn't had any interest in young boys and hadn't asked too many questions. Instead, Michael had given him a place to rest, taught him how to play dominoes, and – most importantly – explained to him about women, what STDs were, and the importance of using condoms. Knowing in his heart that he never wanted to be a father, Silas had taken Michael's advice and had never once gone unprotected when he'd been with a woman.

He'd watched through the years as other men bowed under the costs and pressures of raising children. It wasn't even the money, Silas had come to realize, especially once he'd worked his way into a comfortable position in life. It was the absolute fear that he would turn out to be the type of father his own had been.

Silas was happy with his life as it was. He had a routine he enjoyed, a great dog, and nobody relying on him for anything. He hadn't missed Mirra's invitation last night – he'd deliberately ignored it. There was no space in his life for a woman like Mirra, and he had no interest in contaminating such a perfect being with his own dark issues. She was a gentle ray of sunshine, and Silas was the dark cloud of an impending storm. No matter how strong the pull he felt was, Silas knew he had to stay away from her. For both of their sakes.

"Time to get up, boy. We've got work to do."

An hour later, Silas was drinking a cup of coffee at his captain's desk. Captain Reid had tanned skin, weathered from the sun, and piercing dark eyes that saw everything. He'd been a good mentor to Silas, and most of the crew respected his leadership.

"Good work this week, Silas. Though I'll admit it *was* against protocol to jump into the water and leave your boat."

"I understand, sir. But she was going to die."

"As I said, good work. And we were able to apprehend the illegal fishermen along with their boat, so all in all, an excellent day's work."

"I'm glad to hear it."

"I see Splash has a hero badge." Captain Reid bent to give Splash a treat from the stash he kept in the drawer for the dog.

"Yes, from the woman we saved."

"Where's yours? You deserve one too."

"What else did you want to discuss today?" Silas deftly changed the subject, uncomfortable with the title of hero.

Captain Reid's eyes went serious and Silas straightened in his seat. "We've had a tip. One of the fishermen we captured had his hands in two pots."

Silas raised an eyebrow in question. "Drugs?"

"Exactly. In exchange for reduced charges, he's given us some information on a drug haul coming up from South America. It's big, Silas."

"Cocaine?"

"Yes, and a crap-load of it. It'll be arriving in the next couple of weeks. But we have a problem."

"What's that?"

"Now that they know we've apprehended one of their men, we're going to be in their sights. It'll be easier for them to take us out or get to us than it would be to call off this operation."

"You think we're targets now?"

"I know it, boyo. These are the big guns. This shipment is coming from a highly organized cartel with a lot of money and a lot of firepower. I'm putting you on notice to be on guard the next few weeks. Not just on the water, but on island as well. If they can incapacitate us, even detain us, they'll be able to clear the drop-off here and move it quickly."

"Understood, sir."

"Those around you are in danger, as well. Including Splash. I can't stress this enough – these are bad dudes. We're talking millions of dollars at stake. They will not hesitate to take out anyone who stands in their way."

"Can we get a mole in? Let them think we'll take a cut of it to keep quiet?"

"Hmm." Captain Reid drummed his fingers on the desk. "I'm not certain we'd have time to establish enough trust before this drop is made."

"But maybe it would be because we just caught the fisherman and now caught wind of the drop. And then say that one of us needs money. Make up a story? I'm happy to do it," Silas said.

"Let me think on it. Instinctively, my gut says that's the wrong direction to take with them. I think we just have to be on guard and bring in backup. We've notified the surrounding islands, and we've got a Coast Guard crew coming in next week for extra hands."

"How do you think they'll execute the drop-off?"

"Likely by a barrel drop at night. It would be the most efficient way. It's not as tricky as landing a plane."

"But a plane's not ruled out?"

"No, but they'd have to land at night with no lights."

"That can be done. Down south. It's undeveloped and nobody's down there at night."

"We'll increase patrols that way, but I'm still thinking barrel drop."

"Why?"

"Because the fisherman had been on island for a while before signing on with the boat crew. The rest of the crew wasn't from around here – but he was. Which leads me to believe he was recruited on island to get an in with the locals. The locals aren't going to be much help in landing a plane, but a lot of them – especially the fishermen – know the waters inside and out. Tuck a few high-speed Jet Skis out of the way in one of the caves along the cliffs and they'll recover the barrels quick enough."

"But then where do they take them? It has to go somewhere."

"My guess? Likely to an outer island where they *can* easily land a plane or they've got a boat stashed."

"Won't the satellite pick up a boat?"

"Unless they have a signal jammer."

"So our best bet is to catch them in the act and grab the barrels."

"Right. Interception is ideal. But very, very dangerous. These men will plan for trouble. So until then, you are put on notice: No drinking. No distractions. Anyone and anything around you becomes a liability. Understood?"

"Understood."

"Good. Stay safe out there today. I'll be upping our radio check-ins to hourly until the threat passes. Night shift will be different, but we'll discuss that later. I'll have you continue on days for now."

"Works for me. Happy to help however you need it."

"I know that. You've done a great job here, Silas. I'm lucky to have you on the team."

"Thank you, sir. It's an honor to work with you."

"You hear that, Splash? He's buttering up the boss. Not a bad idea." Captain Reid bent to pat Splash before nodding his dismissal to Silas. Silas whistled for Splash and together they left the office. All thoughts of Mirra had fled.

Silas scanned his surroundings as he walked to the wharf, knowing sleep would be minimal until this drop was over. He trusted Captain Reid, and if the man said he needed to stay alert, he would take those words to heart.

CHAPTER 7

"So he didn't take you up on meeting again?" Jolie inquired. The two sisters were sitting at a long wooden table that was set up under the shade of a few palm trees in their garden. Mirra had brought her paints out, and together the sisters were painting clay pots to put in the garden for their plants. The wind was high today, kicking up little whitecaps on the waves out front, and one lonely pelican divebombed the water in hopes of scoring lunch.

Mirra had piled her hair up on her head and wore a paint-specked apron over her loose linen sheath. Barefoot as usual, she dug her toes into the sand as she contemplated her pot. "Nope. He completely jumped over it."

"I'm sorry," Jolie said, her expression a mixture of sympathy and anger. "Also, what an idiot. Any man would have to be to turn down the chance to spend more time with you."

Mirra laughed gently. "While I appreciate that, not every man is taken with me."

"Most are. Same with me. And that's not even me being cocky. You know how our siren magick works, even when we tone it down. I suspect that for men, it's like smelling cookies or something and they can't have a taste."

"So now I'm a cookie?"

"Absolutely. And there's no reason Silas shouldn't want a bite."

"There's plenty of reasons, I'm sure. He just didn't care to share them."

"Will you dig deeper there? Are you going to give him a push?"

"I think I'm going to have to." Mirra sighed and dug her feet deeper into the sand, the fine grains squelching deliciously between her toes. "I don't see him coming to me anytime soon. And now that I've found him…well, what else am I supposed to do?"

"I'm sure you have a plan."

"I'm thinking of bringing him a plant."

"A plant?" Jolie laughed. "Whatever for?"

"His space just seems so utilitarian. There's nothing that isn't serviceable. No whimsy, no warmth. I suspect he's a guy who sleeps with one pillow and one sheet. It feels like he is just renting the space. It's like he could pack his bag and walk out the door the next morning and be gone."

"Maybe he's had to live that way."

"I suspect he has. He did say this was the longest he'd ever lived anywhere. But if he is settling in, wouldn't he want a few things to warm the place up?"

"What does he like to do for fun?"

"I don't think he does *fun*." Mirra laughed at Jolie's arched brow. "No, really! He said he lives a simple life. Sometimes he plays dominoes with the old men on the corner. Otherwise he comes home from work, reads his books, and has a glass of rum. That's about it. I think routine is probably something that suits him."

"Why not give him a book to read, then? That way he has to return it to you when he's finished."

"That's not really..." Mirra trailed off. "Oh, good point. If I lend him a book, he'll have to bring it back. That's an extra interaction."

"I can't believe we're even having this conversation. I want to go bop this man over the head for not immediately falling for you."

"Ted didn't immediately fall for *you*."

"Yes, he did. It was just his ethics and his own insecurities keeping him from making a move." Jolie smiled the smug smile of a woman confident in her relationship.

"Well, maybe Silas is insecure too."

"You'll have to find out. He strikes me as fairly confident. He didn't bow to Irma's pressure to have dinner, so he definitely has a backbone and doesn't seem to care much for social niceties."

"I'm okay with a man who knows his own mind. I'd just like to understand him better."

"You're certain he's the one the oracle told you about?" Concern flashed over Jolie's pretty face.

"I'm certain. It feels like...like I've come home? I don't know if that's the right way to describe it. But when I saw him, I just realized he was mine. That was it."

"Then take him a book and the plant. See how he responds."

LATER, Mirra felt nerves slide through her as she pulled to a stop at Silas's gate. He might not be home. In that case, she would just leave the book and the plant on the table in his garden. She'd brought him a pot she'd painted in shades of blue, like the ocean at varying depths. In it, she'd tucked a lime tree that was just starting to sprout fruit. Mirra figured he might be more inclined to take care of a plant that produced something useful, like fruit, and lime was always a good addition to rum drinks or food.

"Oh, you're home," Mirra called, smiling to see Silas striding across the garden to her. "I just wanted to stop by and bring you something."

"Why?"

"Because that's who I am as a person," Mirra said with a laugh as she handed the plant to a surprised Silas.

"What is this?"

"It's a lime tree. See? There's two already starting to grow." Mirra pushed the leaves aside to show Silas where the green fruit had just formed at the tip of the branches.

"A lime tree? I have no idea how to take care of a lime tree," Silas said, thrusting it back at her.

Mirra held up her hands and didn't take the pot back. "It's not hard. Just partial shade and water periodically. It'll be fine. I promise."

"But... I don't..." Silas looked from her to the plant, his mouth working, but no words coming out.

"You'll do great with it. I'm sure of it. And if you think it's not doing well, just call me and I'll come take a look."

"I don't have your number."

"We can remedy that." Mirra let the comment hang.

Silas just looked from her to the lime tree and back, clearly at a loss for how to proceed. "But…"

"I painted the pot myself," Mirra volunteered as she slipped inside the gate and bent to pet Splash, who'd come to enthusiastically greet her. "I thought you might like the blue colors since it looks like the ocean and I know you like being on the water."

Finally Silas turned and stomped across the garden, his softly muttered curses floated to her on the evening breezes. Biting back a smile, Mirra patted Splash once more, noticing that Silas had kept the hero badge on the dog's bandana.

"Where am I supposed to put this?" Silas said, looking around his garden with a dismayed expression on his face.

"Well, if you want partial shade, I think it would look nice next to your front door." Mirra pointed to the empty stoop by his door. "And that way you'll pass it every day and think to tend to it."

"Good point." Silas put the pot down and stepped back to study it. "It looks nice there." He sounded as enthusiastic as a person going to the dentist.

"It does," Mirra agreed.

"Well, thanks for stopping by. I really should…" Silas turned and then narrowed his eyes at the book she was holding out to him. "What's this?"

"I'm lending you one of my favorite books."

"I don't need books. I have plenty." Silas held his hands up again.

"But you'll read through them. At some point you'll pick this up, no?"

"What's it about?" Despite himself, Silas came forward and took the book from her hands.

"It's about mermaid myths and legends around the world. I thought that, as a sailor, you might enjoy it. And there's even a chapter on Siren Island in there."

"I'll admit, I do love a good seafaring story. Not to mention mermaids," Silas said. "See?" He held his arm out and turned it to face her. Mirra's eyebrows shot up as she saw an intricately designed mermaid tattooed on his inner arm. She hadn't noticed it before. The design was beautifully done – not in the awkward line styling of a Sailor Jerry-style tattoo, but more involved, with what looked to be Polynesian designs woven through the scales of the tail. But it wasn't the design of the tattoo that gave Mirra pause – it was the fact that the mermaid looked almost exactly like her. Flowing blond hair swirled around the curvy body and she wore a serene expression – a woman at home in her power.

He'd branded himself with Mirra before he'd even met her. Now she had to wonder if he'd ever dreamed of her.

"That's beautiful work. I really love it," Mirra said, and reached out to trace a finger over the design. The moment she touched his skin, a jolt of electricity seemed to leap between them, causing her heart to speed up. Licking her lips, Mirra looked up and caught Silas staring at her face, raw hunger in his eyes.

"Thank you," Silas said, and pulled his arm back, shuttering his eyes.

"So, I hope you'll enjoy the book. You can call me when you finish it or just come by the Laughing Mermaid. One of us is usually around."

"I'll do that. Thanks, Mirra. You don't have to keep stopping by to thank me."

"I'm not just stopping by just to thank you. I'm bringing you gifts of appreciation," Mirra pointed out.

"You already did that with dinner."

"Yes, well, I thought you'd like this too. Am I wrong?"

"No." Silas scrubbed his hand on his face, a gesture Mirra noted he used when he seemed frustrated. "Well, maybe with the lime plant. I'm not sure about that."

"It's okay not to be sure about things. You might end up loving it, though."

"I might. It's hard to say."

Mirra tried to think of something else to say, but it was clear Silas wasn't up for a chat. With nothing left to do – unless she wanted to plop her butt down and refuse to leave – she wandered back to the gate, Splash at her heels.

"I really like Splash. He's a good dog."

"He is. I'm lucky he picked me."

"Did he pick you? Maybe he knew what you needed." Mirra crouched to pet Splash once more before turning to look at Silas.

"And what do you think I need, Mirra?"

"Love," Mirra said simply. She clicked the gate closed, leaving a sullen-looking man behind her.

CHAPTER 8

"*H*e needs a friend," Irma decided. She was standing at the counter, kneading dough for bread.

"I'm trying to be his friend," Mirra said. "But he's very standoffish."

"People who have been hurt a lot in life usually are."

"Maybe he just never learned how to make friends?" Mirra wondered. She reached beneath the table to pat Snowy on the head. Jolie was off with Ted doing some sort of research for another book, and Irma and Mirra had gladly volunteered to watch the dog. He was at the Laughing Mermaid most days anyway, preferring to hang out at the beach and meet up with Pipin for a good run every once in a while. Pipin, their neighbor dog, had taken to Snowy like they were brothers separated at birth.

"I get the sense he's led a hard life, Mirra. Has he spoken to you of his past at all?"

"No, but he did make a comment that he didn't drink a lot because he had to be on guard all the time."

"And why is that?" Irma turned and met Mirra's eyes across the kitchen.

"He said because he's the only one who looks out for himself."

"That's not a grown man talking." Irma pursed her lips. "That's a scared little boy's voice."

"Because a man doesn't have to always look over his shoulder…but a child does." Mirra sighed.

"I wonder what his family life was like growing up?"

"From the very little he's said, I suspect it wasn't great. He eats cold beans from a can."

"He does not." Irma started kneading the bread again, with much more enthusiasm this time. "That sounds like someone who didn't have anyone to care for them."

"He claims it's tasty."

"I'm sure it is. There's nothing inherently wrong with cold beans. It's just a very uninspired way to take your food."

"Not for pleasure but for sustenance."

"Exactly." Irma narrowed her eyes at Mirra. "I think he needs more than a friend. He needs a family."

"I don't know that he'll allow it. Even last night – he didn't offer me a drink. He wasn't interested at all in having me stay around for a chat. I would've had to just sit myself down at the table. If he was interested, wouldn't he at least try to keep me there?"

"I don't think Silas wants attachments in his life."

"So then…what? Do I keep pushing or do I respect that?" Mirra leaned back and took a sip of her coffee. She'd tossed and turned for much of the night. "Like, how would I feel if I had made it clear to a man that I wasn't interested, but he kept showing up with gifts and pestering me? I'd be annoyed and feel frustrated that the man hadn't listened to me. Is it fair that I keep pushing when the situation is reversed? Being feminists means we also have to respect a man's boundaries too."

"You're absolutely right. It's important we be respectful of anyone's boundaries. Has he expressly told you not to come by anymore?"

"Well, he's said not to bring him gifts. He doesn't want any more recognition for his act of heroism."

"Hmm. And you brought him a book to read? But for him to return to you?"

"I did."

"It might be best to just let this sit for a moment." Irma held up a floury hand when Mirra's lips pushed out in a pout. "Love is not a race, my dear. From what I can see, Silas is extremely cautious with people and he likes his routine. You're a disruption to that routine."

"Gee, thanks for the flattering description," Mirra groused.

"But you are. It's not a bad thing. There's no way you haven't gotten into his head. He'll still be worried about you swimming out in the water. He's seen you naked, so that's likely burned into his head. He's talked to you over dinner. While it may not seem like he opened up much, it's certainly a lot for someone like him. I'd say you've dug in. But now is the time for patience, Mirra. This is something he'll need to come to terms with on his own."

"But he's *here*. He's right here!" Mirra bent over and

banged her head on the table. Her stomach was tied in knots just thinking about him, let alone not knowing if he would ever truly see her.

"And he's not going anywhere. You'll also need your own time to adjust to this new idea of having a partner. It'll change your life too. Be gentle with him and yourself, Mirra. It's one of your greatest assets."

"Being gentle? I always thought it was a shortcoming," Mirra sniffed.

"It's not. Particularly when dealing with wounded animals. Silas is wounded. You need to treat him accordingly."

"Give him time," Mirra said, and felt warmth slide through her at getting a better grasp of the situation. If she could train herself to view the virile, strapping man that was Silas as wounded, she would feel more in control. "I can help him heal."

"You can show him love. I don't know his situation, but I'm not sure he's ever had that before. I'd operate under the assumption that he doesn't know the first thing about love."

"That's a sad thing to contemplate."

"Love is a gift, and not everyone is given it. But you have plenty to give and I have faith in you that you can give Silas what he needs."

"A friend."

"Friends first. Build that trust. Love comes later."

"Thank you for being my guiding light. I love you." Mirra went over and embraced Irma, who leaned back into her daughter's arms.

"You're a brilliant shining soul, Mirra. I couldn't be prouder of you and Jolie. Don't fuss too much over Silas. You'll find your way with him."

"I only needed a compass, and you provided that. Thank you. I'm going to go for a swim and clear my head."

"Tell the turtles I said hi."

Mirra laughed watching Snowy dance down the beach with her to the waterline, where he barked at the waves rolling in. Pipin, hearing his bark, came running out and the two began to race across the beach together. Mirra had discarded her cover-up on a chair in the garden, and now dove into the water wearing a scrap of fabric that could technically be called a bathing suit. It was as close as she could get to swimming naked in the sea during the day, when tourists were around.

Mirra swam for a while, smiling down at the fish that swarmed around her. She didn't need a mask to see through the clear Caribbean waters. With barely a cloud in the sky, she could see straight to the bottom, and she loved how the rays of light flickered through the turquoise water. She floated in place for a moment, enjoying the peace that flooded her when she returned to the water, and let herself drift with the gentle current of the sea.

Mirra let her thoughts move to Silas. The ocean knew a thing or two about patience. Over the years its water would smooth the stones on the beach, and its reefs would reclaim damage from destructive humans. There certainly was something to the old adage about going with the flow and letting things work out as they may.

"Your mother is right."

Mirra gasped and blinked at the oracle, who appeared before her in the water. The mermaid's eyes were completely white, matching the opal iridescence of her fin. She floated beneath Mirra, a gentle smile on her lips, her white hair flowing in ribbons around her head.

"Oracle! I've never seen you outside of the city."

"I've come to warn you."

"About Silas? But I thought he was the one you showed me."

"Hush, child, and listen. I have little time."

Obediently, Mirra pressed her lips together and waited for the oracle's reading.

Blue light flashed from the oracle's eyes, and words poured from her. "Your man needs you. Don't turn your back on him – no matter how hard he tries to get you to leave. Your presence is important. This is not just about love. This is about saving his life. Danger comes quickly in the night. He will not be safe unless you intervene. The time to act will be soon. Be bold, my darling Mirra, for love will always conquer all."

"What will happen? Where is this danger coming from?" Mirra asked, her heart racing, but the oracle had already disappeared.

It was highly unusual for the oracle to give a reading like this, and Mirra was lucky she had been given one at all. But now her insides churned as she devoured the oracle's words. If her presence was important, how was she supposed to give Silas space? She needed to protect him from danger – could she do that from afar while gently guiding him into trusting her?

More confused than ever, Mirra turned back to the Laughing Mermaid, her heart in her throat.

As one of her favorite movie characters in *The Big Lebowski* would say: "New shit has come to light."

Now if only she could make sense of it all.

CHAPTER 9

*L*ove. Silas scoffed at the thought as he wandered down the street, Splash at his heels. As far as he was concerned, Silas didn't need anything more in his life to be content. Plus, one had to actually believe in love to know if one needed it, right?

The best he could determine was that love was a societal construct that way too many people bought into and then had their hearts broken when it didn't work out the way it did in the movies. Sure, he knew people who were happy with their partners – but that was companionship. Love, though? He'd be hard-pressed to explain what that emotion actually felt like. Silas had certainly never received it, and he was sure he didn't have it in him to give.

"You look like you're working up a head of mad."

Silas stopped walking and looked over the wall of a garden that enclosed a small fisherman's hut. Prince – the owner, and a local who had his hand in a bit of everything on island – beamed his gap-toothed grin at him.

"Prince. Good to see you, man. How goes it?"

"Oh, it goes, it goes." The old man rocked back on the small stool he sat on, wrinkles creasing his dark skin, his hair a shock of white that stood up in little tufts. "Just flowing like de ocean, man."

"Seems the best way to be," Silas said, leaning on the gate.

"Come in, come in. You've got time to sit with an old man."

"You'll outlive us all, Prince, of that I'm certain."

"Sure and dat's because of my good livin'." Prince slapped his leg and laughed. "Love of a good woman, fresh air, and taking life as it comes."

"I'll take the second two, you can have the first," Silas grumbled as he entered the garden. He pulled up a chair next to the small table where Prince was already opening his box of dominoes.

"Nah, you've got it de wrong way, man." Prince chuckled and shook his head, slapping the white blocks onto the table. "Love is all dat matters."

Silas shrugged. "If you believe in it."

"Ach, come on, man – you can't tell me you don't believe in love?" Prince stared at him, aghast, and then clicked his tongue. "Shame."

"I won't deny you've got yourself a good woman," Silas said. Maria, Prince's wife was a sweet, yet formidable woman.

"She's de best thing dat ever happened to me. You'll know when you find yours." Prince bent to pet Splash. "Now, would you look at dis? Does Splash have a hero pin? What did dis brave fellow do?"

"It's quite a story."

"I've got de time."

Frowning, Silas concentrated on the game as he relayed the story. Prince stayed silent during the retelling of it, nodding occasionally as he added another tile to the board.

"And Mirra awarded Splash his fancy new badge. I didn't have it in my heart to not let him wear it. He's very proud of himself."

"As he should be. Manning de boat while you throw yourself overboard like a fool."

"Wasn't much else to be done. Was I supposed to let her die?"

"Naw, man, you did de right thing, dat's de truth." Prince rubbed his chin as he studied the tiles on the table before making his next move. "Hell of a woman, dat Mirra is. All de ladies at de Laughing Mermaid."

"Yes, I can see that. They're knockouts."

"More than just beauty." Prince looked up and met Silas's eyes. "Brains and power too."

"They pack a punch, that's for sure."

"Dat Mirra, though – you should take her to dinner."

"What is everyone's obsession with going to dinner?" Silas wondered, propping his elbows on his knees as he studied the board.

"It's a common thing in society, you know. We gather for food. We laugh. Maybe dance a little. Have fun. Perhaps you've heard of it? Having fun?"

Silas shrugged and moved a tile.

"Ah, de man doesn't have time for fun, is dat it?"

"Listen, my life didn't always allow for a lot of downtime. I've been working sixteen-to-eighteen-hour days since I was a teenager."

"You don't be working dat hard now. I see you walking Splash. Playing dominoes. You have more time."

"I do. But I like my routine. Read my books, have a little food, maybe a glass of rum. It's a simple life, but one that's good for me."

"A woman would be good for you."

"Why? Women cause problems. They'll only shake up my routine. I'm good now."

"Are you?" Prince laughed as he finished destroying Silas in the game. "Look at dat. You ain't paying any attention. I think dis woman got in your brain. See, dat's de problem with women, man…you say you don't want them, but they're sneaky. They get inside." Prince tapped his temple.

"They don't… I'm not…" Silas sighed as Prince just stared him down. "Okay, I'll admit that my thoughts wander to Mirra on occasion. She gave me a freakin' plant. What am I supposed to do with a plant?"

"What kind of plant?" Prince demanded, stacking up the domino tiles.

"A lime tree."

"Ah, smart woman. A flower would put you off. Limes? Dat's a useful gift. You'll take care of it." It wasn't a question.

"Yes, I'll take care of it. Now she has me researching the care of lime trees and I'm fussing over the damn thing every day in case it gets sick."

"See? I tell you. Dey get in your head."

"I'm going to return her book and that will be the last of it."

"Sho, and you can't be thinking dat'll be de end of dat?" Prince slapped his scrawny leg again and laughed. "What book did she bring you?"

"One on mermaid myths and legends."

"Bet you read it already, didn't you?"

Silas sighed and squeezed the bridge of his nose. "It was a good book."

"What you think about those mermaids? You like dem?"

"Of course. Any sailor worth his salt likes mermaids."

"Your tattoo looks just like her." Prince pointed to Silas's arm as he began to lay out tiles again.

"What?" Silas looked down at the ink on his arm and studied his mermaid more closely. "Damn it. You're right." Now that he'd met Mirra and had seen her voluptuous body in the water, her blond hair rioting around her head, he'd never be able to unsee her in the design of his tattoo.

"Why you get dat tattoo?"

"I, uh, well…" Silas felt a little foolish, but this was Prince and the man was an absolute trove of secrets. "I actually had it done after I had a dream. It was that dream that made me look up Siren Island."

"What was de dream about?"

Silas could still remember it as vividly as if he had dreamed it the night before. He'd been sinking into darkness, the water seeming to suck him deeper and deeper. Even though he logically knew he was in danger, his mind had been at peace with it. Perhaps it had been a reflection of that time in his life, where little mattered but keeping his head down and making his next buck, but in his dream Silas had been willing to let it all go.

However, as he sank, from the inky depths a light had appeared. Not blinding like a flashlight, more of an ethereal glow that soothed as much as it beckoned. Silas had kicked toward it, only to discover the most beautiful mermaid he'd ever seen swimming toward him, a gentle smile on her face. Only now, as he revisited the dream and the way she'd wrapped her arms around him, pressing a kiss to his lips and breathing air into his lungs, did Silas realize she was a dead ringer for Mirra.

In fact, she *was* Mirra.

Shocked, Silas rocked back on his chair, almost toppling over as the flimsy legs bowed in the gravel.

"Dat sounds like Mirra," Prince affirmed, flashing a smile at him. "She called to you from afar."

"That's ridiculous," Silas scoffed. But the rightness of Prince's statement settled into his core.

"Might be. Dat doesn't change de truth of it," Prince said, studying the table again as they began the next game. "I would think dat after all your time on de water, you know not everything can be explained."

"I know that. I've seen some...odd things." Silas shrugged and moved a tile.

"So? She called to you. It's Siren Island we live on, man, what do you think?"

"I don't think that Mirra called to me years ago and I uprooted my whole life to come here because of her."

"Maybe not, maybe so. Why you come here then?"

"I..." Silas narrowed his eyes at Prince. "You gonna play, old man, or just talk all day?"

"Dat's what I thought!" Prince crowed. "I can talk and play at de same time."

"Mmm." Silas decided to change the subject as he wasn't comfortable with where the conversation was going. "Prince…you hear anything on the water? Talk among the fishermen?"

"'Bout what now?" Prince raised his chin to look at Silas.

"It's about a drop."

"I hear things. Not all good." Prince shrugged.

"Do me a favor, would you?"

"Depends." Ever cautious, Prince waited.

"Take care of yourself. Don't get involved. Don't let anyone you care about get involved. These are bad dudes. Not worth your life."

"You know I don't be playing in dat. Dirty money. I like an honest day's work, dat's de truth."

"I know it. But people trust you and you know everyone on island. I've been warned. So I'm passing that on to you."

"When is dis happening?"

"Soon. Keep your people close. Keep safe."

"Seems to me you'd be the one needing to keep safe."

"I know about it. They don't know we've been tipped off. Although – they have eyes everywhere, so maybe they do know by now."

"Dey try to intimidate me, dey've got another think coming," Prince said.

"I think they'll want an in with the locals. And they'll come after any law enforcement." Silas knew one of Prince's sons worked at the police station.

"Thanks for de tip. I'll get de word out."

"If you hear anything of use…"

"I'll find you. But only if you promise me something."

"What's that?"

"Be good to Mirra. She's de best I know. I say handle with care."

"I'm not handling at all, so she'll be just fine." Silas whistled to Splash and left the garden with a wave.

"Stupid man." Prince shook his head and stacked the dominoes back in their box. "He don't know what he's missing. But he'll find out. Oh, yes he will. Love has a way of claiming you for a dance."

CHAPTER 10

*T*he universe had a way, Mirra thought with a
small smile as she watched Silas plod toward
her with Splash at his feet. She took a moment to observe
him without his notice. Anyone looking at him would see a
badass dude, she realized. His face was set in fierce lines,
the edge of his jaw sharp. The tattoos decorating his arms
added to the image, and he carried himself with the air of a
man who could handle anything that came his way. His
eyes were doing a perpetual scan, and she saw the moment
he noticed her, watched as his step faltered briefly, as
though he was deciding whether to turn around or not.
When she smiled at him, Silas seemed to come to a decision and moved her way.

Spying Mirra, Splash raced down to where she sat at a
picnic table under a palm tree on the beach. She'd come to
town today to visit the shops, but couldn't resist the lure of
the sunshine and pretty blue water. As a reward for doing
the marketing, Mirra had planned to get herself some
gelato and people-watch for a while.

"Hi, Splash! Aren't you a good doggo?" Mirra bent to pet the enthusiastic dog, happy to see he still wore his hero badge. Splash seemed to agree with her, and wriggled with joy at seeing her.

"Hello, Mirra," Silas said.

"Hello, Silas." Mirra tilted her head up at him and smiled, a long pull of heat rushing through her at his nearness. Did he feel the same when he was close to her?

"I wish I'd known I would bump into you today. I would have brought the book with me."

Mirra translated that to mean he was annoyed that now he would have to make a separate trip to visit her to return the book. She bit back a smile. "Did you read it already? I'm glad you were able to find the time."

"It's hard to resist a good mermaid story."

"Care to join me? I'm just waiting until the line dwindles, then I'm going to grab a gelato from the stand."

Splash settled at her feet, seeming to make the decision for Silas. He looked from the dog to her.

"I guess," Silas said after a pause. "What can I get for you?"

"Oh, I can get it..." Mirra trailed off as Silas just looked at her. "Right. I'll take pistachio, please."

"Really? Not chocolate or caramel or something?"

"Nope. Pistachio's the best."

"If you say so. I'll be right back. Splash, stay."

The dog seemed perfectly content to do so, his little paw resting on Mirra's foot as they both watched Silas walk to the gelato stand and wait at the window. The man really was all muscle, Mirra thought, trying to tamp down the heat that rushed through her. If she hadn't been in so much pain when he'd rescued her, she would have been able to appreciate his strong arms around her. It had been a little hard to focus on anything else when she was conserving all her power for trying to heal her wounds.

"He needs love, Splash. I don't think he realizes just how much. You do a good job of giving it to him, though, don't you?" Mirra murmured, bending over to scratch Splash's ears.

"Here you go," Silas said, arriving back at the table and dropping onto the bench next to her. "I didn't know if you'd want a cone or a dish, so I went with cone."

"Good choice. Less waste as well." Mirra smiled and licked a drop of gelato that had already begun to melt down the side of the cone. Silas froze for a moment, watching her, and then deliberately turned to the dog. Aha, Mirra thought, not so unaffected by her, then.

"They had your doggo cone too, Splash." Silas held out a dog bone treat with a little puff of whipped cream on top. The dog jumped up and took it delicately from Silas's hands before settling himself back into the sand to devour his treat.

"Now isn't that darling?" Mirra laughed. "I never would have thought of that. They don't miss a trick."

"Lots of people walk their dogs on this beach."

"Was it free?"

"No, a small charge. Which is smart, because dog people are crazy and will usually buy anything for their pups."

"Are you a crazy dog dad then?" Mirra laughed. "Do you have matching robes and a pillow with his name on it?"

A faint flush tinged Silas's cheeks, delighting Mirra. "Not robes," he muttered, and focused on his own cone.

"I'm sorry, what was that? I must have missed what you said."

"He has a dog bed with his name on it, okay? But not matching robes or anything crazy like that." Silas glowered at her.

"An embroidered dog bed is totally normal. Does he like it?" Silence greeted her, and Mirra's smile widened. "I'm guessing that means he skips the dog bed and sleeps with you."

"Damn dog. I swear, you buy them the nice stuff and they ignore it. I could buy him a fancy stuffed toy and he'd go for a leftover hunk of rope from my boat."

"Kind of like cats that way," Mirra said with a laugh. "You buy them something and they just want to play in the bag you got it in or sit in the box."

"Cats," Silas scoffed.

"Not a cat fan?"

"Not really. Do you have them?"

"Nope, just shared custody of my sister's dog. But I like all animals," Mirra said. "Don't you want to try some of my horrible pistachio?" She held her cone out to Silas.

"It's green," Silas said, wrinkling his nose at her cone.

"And?"

"Sweets should not be green. They should be chocolate."

"Ah, a purist, I see." Mirra held her cone where it was. "Are you scared, then?"

"Of course not," Silas said. He swapped cones with her, and they each took a lick.

"Chocolate and peanut butter. Good choice," Mirra said. She watched him as confusion flooded his face before he scowled down at her cone. "Well?"

"It…" Silas pressed his lips together.

Mirra traded cones with him again, barely holding back a laugh. "You like it, don't you?"

"Damn it. Yes. I wasn't expecting a green dessert to be that good." Silas let a smile slip and it warmed Mirra straight to her core. The man needed more laughter in his life.

Mirra smirked. "If I weren't such a good person, I would say 'I told you so.' However, I'll refrain from doing so."

"It still kinda feels like you did," Silas pointed out.

"Did I? Imagine that."

"Fine, you win. Pistachio is damn good and I might even order it the next time I think to get gelato."

"Do you come down here often?" Mirra asked, watching a mom hook the arm of a fat-bottomed toddler and wade into the water. "I'm surprised I ran into you, considering that despite how long I've lived here, I've never seen you before."

Silas shrugged. "Maybe you have and just didn't notice me."

"I highly doubt that. You make quite an impression," Mirra said, trying out some light flirtation to see how he would respond.

"Not like you do. I'm surprised every man on the beach wasn't crowded around begging to buy you gelato when I saw you."

Well, then, Mirra thought. He clearly appreciated her looks. "You must have scared them off."

"Wimps," Silas said, causing Mirra to throw her head back and laugh. "That's some laugh you have there, Miss Mirra."

"Is it? I wouldn't know. It's just mine."

"It sounds like wind chimes in a gentle breeze."

"My...that's a very romantic depiction." Mirra tilted her head to him.

"I can be poetic at times, I guess. Must be all that reading." Silas shrugged one shoulder and looked back out to the water. Now the toddler sat on his butt slapping the water with his hands, while his mother tried to coat him with sunscreen. A howl greeted her attempts, and Mirra chuckled.

"You want kids?" Silas asked, surprising Mirra.

"I think so," Mirra said, studying the furious child, "but I'm not so certain. I think that as long as I have the right partner, I'll be happy with my life either way."

"You aren't happy now? On your own?" Silas demanded.

"I am content right now. I enjoy my family and my life. But I do know there's a piece missing." *You*, Mirra silently added.

"How can you be so certain? What if your best days are now and you don't realize it until later on when you're saddled with some guy you end up resenting and a kid who sucks the lifeblood out of you?"

"Well, now where did the romantic go?" Mirra laughed at Silas, and then saw his face was serious. "To answer your question, I suppose there are no guarantees in life. I'd like to think I'd pick the right partner for myself so I wouldn't grow to resent him. As for whether I'd birth a parasite-like child, I really can't say. I haven't thought too deeply about that aspect of life. Seems a bit like putting the cart before the horse."

"I don't want kids." Silas bit the words out, and Mirra knew she had to tread carefully. She took a moment and continued to enjoy her cone.

"It's good to know what you want."

"I want you to know that about me. I don't know what you're thinking…with me, I mean. That I'm like a knight in shining armor or something because I saved you. But I'll tell you something, princess – I'm no hero to rescue you from your tower."

"I don't recall asking for one," Mirra said, her tone frosty as she shot him a glare.

"Good. Just…don't get any ideas. I like my life as it is and I don't want kids." Finishing his ice cream, Silas stood. Splash automatically joined him. "If you think I'm fresh meat for your dating pool or something, you're dead wrong."

"Well, isn't that sweet?" Mirra smiled at him. "And here I thought we were going to manage to have a nice conversation."

"Just…it's best you leave me be." With that, Silas stomped away, his shoulders hunched as he shook his head, seeming to have a conversation with himself.

"That was certainly illuminating," Mirra murmured to herself. She knew he was deliberately pushing her away for whatever reason. But she'd be lying if she said it didn't sting a bit.

"The good things in life never come easily," Mirra reminded herself, staring after the man who had bought a pup-cone for his dog. "I'll break through your walls eventually."

CHAPTER 11

*I*t had been stupid of him to relax, even for a moment, Silas berated himself as he strode home. People seemed to sense his energy and cleared the path as they saw him coming. Splash, his ever-faithful companion, stuck by his side instead of racing ahead.

Hadn't the captain specifically ordered him to be vigilant? To take care with people close to him? And here he was having ice cream with Mirra in a very public place. He might as well have put a bullseye on her forehead.

Furious with himself, Silas scanned the marina for anything out of the norm. If he was being honest with himself, it wasn't just because of the drug cartel that he'd gone cold with Mirra. For a brief moment, watching the mother play with the toddler in the water, his mind had flashed to Mirra doing that with their son. *Their son.* He'd never thought that way with any woman before. Ever. The thought alone had been like throwing a bucket of ice-cold water over his head, and even though he was aware he was being rude, Silas did what he always did when anyone started to peek over his walls – he left.

He couldn't decide if he was more upset at the fact that he'd put Mirra at risk, or the fact that for the first time in his life he'd gotten an impression that he might enjoy being a father. It was contrary to all he'd promised himself and the carefully constructed world he had built.

A child was a burden. That was that, Silas reminded himself. He'd done his best to build a life where he didn't owe anyone anything, where he had no responsibilities to others. He'd learned a long time ago that children were not a gift, but an anchor.

Some would say a sailor needed an anchor for his boat. But the way Silas saw it, an anchor wasn't just something that would keep him in place – it could also drown him. The overwhelming responsibilities of fatherhood and of being a reliable partner to a wife – well, that was like looking at the wall of a tsunami right before it crashed over his head and took him under.

Sure, he'd been rude to Mirra, but in the end he was only doing her a favor. Her interest in him would have to die now, as Silas could never be the partner that Mirra likely hoped he would be. Silas had trained himself to fly solo and never depend on anyone.

He hadn't missed her signals. It wasn't as though he was blind to cues from women; he had enjoyed his fair share of women in his bed. But a woman like Mirra deserved far more than a quick tumble, and it was best that he kept his distance.

Damn, but he wanted to kiss her.

Silas sighed and cursed under his breath. He'd never

met anyone who'd delivered such a punch to his gut. Mirra was the total package. Softly rounded lips that begged to be kissed, a curvy body that many men would beg to touch, and a laugh that sent shivers across his body. Not to mention she enjoyed reading, Splash loved her, and she genuinely seemed like a kind woman.

A brave one, too.

What woman would risk her life cutting dolphins out of a fishing net? It still shook him when he replayed the image of her caught in the steel cable. It had been seriously stupid, yet incredibly courageous. He could identify with her motives, while also hating that she had put herself on the line like that. It still made his stomach flip to think what might have been lost.

He couldn't be a partner to Mirra, that was for certain, but he'd do his damnedest to make sure he kept her safe from afar.

You own my soul now.

Her words drifted back to him, and Silas shook his head. That was...well, it was just ridiculous. A favor was a favor. He wasn't duty-bound to this woman, and he certainly didn't own her soul. What kind of person even said things like that?

Arriving at his home, Silas paused, his senses on alert.

Something was off.

Scanning the yard, he waited patiently to see if there was any movement – any hint of anything. When nothing happened, he opened the door and stepped inside cautiously. Splash ran over to his water dish. Only when Silas followed did he see the knife stuck through the center of the mermaid book he'd left on the table in the garden. A piece of paper had been pierced through at the top.

Back off.

Silas didn't touch the book. Instead he did a perimeter check of the garden and his house, his switchblade in hand. Once he was certain everything was clear, he returned to the book and took out his phone to take photos of it before placing a call.

"Captain? We've got a problem."

After securing the book in a plastic bag, Silas gave Splash his dinner and went to change his clothes. Had there been something significant about the drug cartel putting a knife through the book Mirra had given him? Or had it been a random choice because it was the only thing of importance sitting out in his garden? It wouldn't have taken much time to slip into the garden and leave the note – perhaps only a matter of a minute. But Silas couldn't help but feel like they'd threatened Mirra as well.

"Damn it." Silas grabbed his keys and headed back out into the kitchen, where Splash sat by the door, ready for his next adventure. Silas briefly debated leaving him at home, but knew he would only worry more. Splash would be safe with him, or he could leave him at the office. His house had been breached already, so leaving his dog behind would only be offering the cartel an opportunity. He could never do that to Splash.

"Come on, boy, we're going for a ride."

Cheerful as always, Splash bounded into Silas's pickup truck and they made their way to the offices at the marina. Silas parked in his designated spot and soon they were in the captain's office.

"I want you on patrol," Captain Reid said without preamble, after Silas had handed him the bag with the book and the knife. "I'll need to keep this for a bit."

"Yeah, but I'd like the book back at some point. It's not mine."

"It's evidence for now. I'm sorry."

"I understand."

"Head to the south. There's a beach there with a cave system. Have a look if you can. You should be able to dock at the mooring and have a swim in. If you leave the boat, I want you checking in with me every ten minutes."

"Do you anticipate trouble?"

"I don't suspect this will be their drop point. It isn't easy to access by foot or car, which would hinder their getaway – unless they don't care if their men on land get caught. It would seem silly not to consider that a problem, though; anyone who gets caught will start talking as soon as they realize they're facing prison. But in any case, I'd feel better if we check it off the list of potential drop sites."

"What's the safety level regarding Splash?"

"I think you're fine to take him with you on this run. As I said, based on the ocean currents and the difficult beach access on that side, it's not likely this will be a consideration. However, when I send you to the higher risk spots, I expect you'll keep him in the office."

"I will. He's important to me, sir."

"And to me. We'll take care of our boy. In fact..." Captain Reid nodded to a package on the table behind Silas. "That just came for Splash."

"What is it?" Silas opened the bag and pulled out a dark dog harness that looked more like a life jacket.

"It's bulletproof and it's a flotation device. Genius, really."

"I had no idea this was a thing," Silas said, relief seeping through him.

"Neither did I. Until this is over, he'll wear it if he's on rounds with you."

"Of course. Thank you for thinking of him." Silas met Captain Reid's eyes. "It means a lot."

"We protect our men – right, Splash?" Captain Reid bent and scratched Splash's ears to cover his embarrassment.

Once on the water, Silas considered the captain's words. As much as he abhorred having a responsibility to anyone, he supposed he'd still managed to create a life where structure and responsibility – as well as brotherhood – mattered. Had he managed to form a family unit in his own way?

Uncomfortable with the thought, Silas rubbed a hand over his heart as he steered the boat to the mooring at the southernmost beach on Siren Island. The captain had been right in his assessment – while the beach was private, it would take the better part of an afternoon to hike to it from land. If the cartel was looking for land support, this would be a tricky spot, not to mention the difficulty with the tides and the prominent reef system in the shallows.

Catching the mooring line with the hook, Silas tied the boat off and paused to study the beach. High cliff walls sheltered the small sandy cove, and the tide was out, meaning more rocks were exposed from the depths of the ocean. A light wind brushed his cheeks, and the sun dipped low on the horizon. He'd need to get in and get out quickly so as to be back on the boat before he lost the light.

"Ready for a swim, boy?" The vest had fit Splash perfectly and he didn't seem to mind wearing it.

Silas radioed into headquarters. "Heading to the beach for a quick land assessment, sir."

He moved to the back platform and dove in, turning to watch as Splash did the same. The dog seemed enthused by the life vest and paddled easily to him. Together, they quickly made their way to shore and climbed from the water. Splash immediately took off to race around the beach, doing the little zoomie dance of a dog who was having fun, and Silas trotted to the edge of the cliff base to begin his surveillance. Moving quickly, he wound his way along the rocks, looking for recent footprints, trash, or any sign of human disturbance. Finding none, he glanced up when Splash signaled with an alarm bark.

Racing over to Splash, Silas surveyed the water and turned full circle to look at the cliffs above. Nothing out of the ordinary jumped out at him. Perhaps Splash was just barking at a crab or something, Silas thought, and dropped to his knees where the dog stood on point.

"What's up, buddy? Did you find a crab? I know you love chasing them."

Splash whined and dug at the sand with his paw.

"Okay, I'll take a look."

Amused, Silas scooped up sand with his hands. When something glimmered in the fading light, he tilted his head at his palms.

Shock wove through him and he looked down at Splash, who seemed to grin up at him expectantly.

It was a pearl.

A miraculous one, at that, if Silas was any judge. About the size of a dime, it was oddly shaped – almost like a bean – and glowed with the luster of the moon.

In seconds, Silas knew what he had to do with it.

"Good job, buddy!" Checking his watch and seeing that he was reaching his ten-minute time limit, Silas secured the pearl in one of his pockets that had a zip closure, and motioned for Splash to follow him back into the water.

Now he had the perfect thing to keep one very determined woman away.

It was time to give Mirra her soul back.

CHAPTER 12

*M*irra had just taken a nibble of the fresh green pepper she was chopping for a salad, the tang of the vegetable sharp in her mouth, when their doorbell rang. Jolie was off with Ted, so it was just Irma and Mirra in the kitchen tonight, and they were making an easy dinner of soup and salad.

"I'll get it," Irma said, wiping her hands on a dish-towel, her turquoise dress flowing behind her as she left the kitchen before Mirra could respond. Mirra continued to chop, swaying her hips to the bouncy reggae beat that throbbed from the little speaker perched on the windowsill.

It had been several days since Mirra had last spoken to Silas, but that didn't mean she hadn't seen him. She'd taken to the water most nights, following his boat as he'd patrolled. Of course, she'd been careful not to let him see her, but Splash hadn't missed her. A smart dog, she thought with a smile. Mirra knew something was up, as Silas had been taking more night shifts lately and there was an air of tension around him. It had to be the danger that the oracle had warned her about. Unsure how to keep Silas safe, all Mirra could do was monitor his movements from afar.

"Really, it's fine. I just wanted to drop something off."

Mirra's head shot up at Silas's voice as Irma all but shoved the man into the kitchen ahead of her. Splash raced across the tiled floor to Mirra, and she crouched to pet the dog who showered her with kisses.

"That's a good boy," Mirra said, taking a moment with Splash to calm the nerves that skittered through her stomach. Standing, she smiled at Silas, who stood uncomfortably in the kitchen, his eyes doing the perpetual scan of his environment.

"Silas. It's nice to see you," Mirra said.

"Hi, Mirra. I just wanted to drop something off for you." Silas had a small bag in his hands.

"Have you eaten?" Irma asked, moving to the jar on the counter where she kept dog treats for Snowy and Pipin.

"No, but –"

"You'll stay for dinner then." It was an order, not a question.

"No, it's fine. I just wanted to drop off…" Silas trailed off as Irma turned and stared him down. "Right. Um, a quick bite then. I really shouldn't stay long."

"Why is that?" Irma asked, her look unwavering.

"It's…it's just. It's…" Silas looked like a deer in headlights as he tried to come up with an answer.

"I'm sure he has a reasonable explanation about why he has to be somewhere else," Mirra interrupted smoothly as she transferred all her salad ingredients into a bowl. "Does soup and salad suit you?"

"Of course," Silas said automatically.

"Can I get you a beer, Silas? Or pour you some wine?"

"No alcohol for me tonight," Silas said. "Water is fine."

"Bubbly or regular?"

"Oh, um, regular," Silas said, and for the first time a faint smile crossed his face.

"Have a seat." Mirra nodded to the long table, hoping to ease some of the tension that was radiating off of Silas.

He shouldn't look this good, Mirra decided, even though she could see the dark circles shrouding his eyes. He wore dark cargo pants and a fitted navy shirt, and it took everything in Mirra's power not to go over and wrap her arms around him. She wanted to feel the strength of his arms cocooning her once again like they had when he'd rescued her.

Silas begrudgingly took a seat at the end of the long wooden dinner table on the other side of the kitchen. Mirra brought the bowl of salad over, and then returned to set the dishes on the table.

"I can help," Silas said, beginning to rise from his chair.

"Sit," Mirra said. She pressed her hand to his shoulder, gently nudging him back into his chair, and felt that lovely warm electric current pulse through her hand. Oh yes, this man was for her. All of her magick recognized his nearness as easily as if it were a key fitting into a lock.

"Tell me, Silas, have you been working a lot lately?" Irma asked, bringing over a bowl of black bean soup. She placed the bowl in front of Silas, along with a thick crust of bread and a small bowl of butter.

"I…yes, I have been." Silas didn't offer anything further; he just waited in silence until the others joined him at the table.

Irma shot Mirra a questioning glance, but she only smiled. Conversations with Silas could be a bit like pulling teeth – it was almost as if the man was out of practice. She supposed long days alone on a boat could do that to a person.

"Salad?" Mirra asked, holding the bowl out.

"Yes. I mean, yes, please," Silas said, and took the bowl from her.

"It sounds like we might get a bit of weather in the next few days," Irma offered, switching to a topic everyone could talk about.

"We might. Will that affect your guests?" Silas asked.

Irma looked relieved at his question. "It's low season right now, so we only have a lovely couple in house. They're on their honeymoon, so I don't think much will disturb them. In fact, a rainy day may be just the excuse they need to stay inside." Irma laughed.

"Is it weird to share your house with other people?" Silas asked, breaking off a piece of the bread and dipping it in his soup.

"It can be," Mirra said, bringing Silas's gaze to hers. "But you know how houses are built here. Concrete walls…you can rarely hear anyone. We've gotten used to the flow of having people around. However, at the end of high season we always close for a week or two just to have a break."

"It's kind of like when you were in school and couldn't wait for summer break," Irma said, looking at Silas.

"I hated summer break," Silas said, and a look of shock crossed his face before he clamped his lips shut.

"Did you? I suppose not all children enjoy the freedom of break. Was it because you enjoyed your classes so?" Irma asked.

"School was my break," Silas said, and shrugged one shoulder.

Irma shot Mirra a quick look when Silas bent his head to his soup again.

"I always liked school," Mirra rushed in. "It was so fun to learn about different worlds or different ways of thinking. I guess I've always liked learning new things. I feel like every time I open a book, it's kind of the same."

"Reading isn't school, though. It's an escape." Silas glanced at her, and Mirra's heart filled with compassion for the little boy who had needed to hide.

"It can be an escape, I agree. It can also be a gift and a joy. Do you read now to escape?" Mirra asked.

Silas took his time thinking about the answer, something Mirra appreciated, and she took a sip of wine as she studied him. This man had been hurt, badly, and it was going to take a lot to charm her way through his defenses. All she wanted to do was pull him into her arms and kiss away all his troubles.

"I haven't thought about it that way in quite a while," Silas finally said. "I guess that means I don't use it for an escape anymore. I read for entertainment now."

"What kinds of books do you like, Silas?" Irma asked.

"Everything, really. I'm partial to a high seas tale, I'll admit. But they often make me angry." Silas laughed, and

Mirra's heart stuttered as warmth flooded his handsome face.

"Why is that?" Irma asked.

"Because nobody gets the details right. You have people writing about sailing rough waters when they've never stepped foot on a boat. They don't really understand currents, or the mood of the ocean, or even how crucial the tides are. It's mistakes like that which pull me out of a story because then I'm like, 'No sailor in their right mind would ever do this!' I have to remind myself it's fiction sometimes."

"But don't you think a good story should pull you along so you don't focus on the minute details?" Mirra asked.

"I'll admit, some stories hook me so much that I don't mind the inaccuracies. I kind of push them to the side because I have to see if he wins the battle."

"That's a good story then," Mirra agreed.

Irma's phone rang from its spot near the kitchen sink. She stood and answered, and then put the phone to her chest. "It's the coordinator for the group that wanted to come next month. This call will take a while. I'm just going to take my soup with me to my office. Silas, it was nice to see you again. Please stop by any time. I always make too much food and I love it when handsome men join my table."

Silas stilled when Irma bent and pressed a kiss to his cheek before picking up her soup and disappearing from the room.

"Does that happen a lot?" Silas asked.

"Interruptions?"

"Yes."

"It's the name of the game in customer service. You get used to it. For the most part, it's stuff we already have the answers written out to. I copy and paste a lot of emails because we get a lot of the same questions."

"The place looks nice. I can see why people would want to stay here," Silas said, looking through the window at the beach.

"I can give you a tour, if you'd like?" Mirra asked.

"I don't have time."

"Okay." Mirra shrugged and took a spoonful of her soup.

"Sorry, that sounded rude." Silas sighed and scrubbed a hand over his face. "Listen, I have to tell you something but it needs to be kept quiet. Can I trust you?"

"With your life," Mirra promised, her eyes meeting his. A haunted look passed through Silas's eyes, just for a moment, and then his cool stare returned.

"I brought you this back, but unfortunately I've had to order you a new one," Silas reached into the bag he'd placed on the chair next to him and pulled out the book she'd given him.

"Why did you have to buy a new one?" Mirra asked, taking it from him. But as soon as she touched the book, Mirra could tell why. Danger surrounded it, as did evil intentions.

"It was stabbed." Silas pointed to the slit in the cover.

Mirra opened the book and paged through it, noting the cut that sliced through all the pages.

"That's quite a knife," Mirra determined.

"It is. And it was left behind, which means the person didn't care about the cost of losing it."

"A villain with money."

"That's correct. A drug cartel, to be exact. I took the long way here and backed over myself quite a bit to lose any tails. But I'm being watched because a big drop is coming up. They thought to threaten me away with a cheerful note."

That explained the danger the oracle had told her about, and why Silas had started doing more night patrols.

"So my book was an unfortunate victim to a drug cartel?" Mirra couldn't help but laugh. "I suppose if a book has to be ruined, that's a much better story than me spilling a cup of coffee on it."

Despite himself, Silas smiled. "This is serious, Mirra."

"I understand, Silas. I could sense you were in danger."

"How?" Silas furrowed his brow.

"I...I don't know. I just could feel it," Mirra shrugged.

"I can't see you anymore, Mirra. Everyone around me is a target right now."

Realization dawned on Mirra. "That's why you were so rude the other day."

"I wasn't..." Silas sat back in the chair and crossed his arms over his chest. Mirra almost drooled; the action made his muscles pop.

"You were."

"Fine – yes, I was rude. I forgot myself for a moment. I don't want to put a target on your head, Mirra. I've already saved your life once. I don't want to be responsible for putting you in danger."

"But –"

"In fact, I have something else for you," Silas said, plowing ahead. He reached for the bag and handed it over to Mirra.

"What's this?" Mirra felt warmth flood through her as she peeked into the bag and saw a small box wrapped in silver paper.

"Open it," Silas bit out.

"A gift? That's very sweet of you." Mirra drew out the box and set aside the bag.

"You don't even know what it is yet."

"Still. It's wrapped nicely, so I hardly think it's going to be a tarantula that leaps out at me."

Silas laughed again, and the tension eased a bit as Mirra carefully peeled back the paper. "Not one to rip the paper off?"

"No, that's my sister, Jolie. I think gifts matter and people should take care when they open them. What about you? Are you a ripper or do you go slow?"

"I...don't know," Silas shrugged. A flicker of embarrassment ran over his face, and Mirra quickly surmised he rarely received gifts. No wonder he'd balked at her giving him a lime tree.

"Did the lime tree survive the attack?" Mirra asked, quickly changing the subject.

"It did. And I have three more limes sprouting." Silas shook his head in disbelief. "Can you believe that? About the size of a quarter." He held up his hand to show her the size.

"That's great. It means you're doing a good job taking care of it."

"I don't much know what I'm doing. It seems happy, though. I've told Splash not to pee on it."

"That's a good thing," Mirra laughed. Splash came to the table at the sound of his name, and she added, "You're a smart dog, Splash."

Splash eyed her hopefully.

"Do you want to get him another treat? There's more in the container on the counter."

"I can't say no to that. He deserves it." Silas stood and crossed the kitchen, Splash at his heels, while Mirra studied the box in her hands. It was a small hinged wooden box with a carving of a wave on the top.

"Is this from Prince?" Mirra held the box up. "He makes boxes like this."

"Yes, it is." Silas returned to the table and dropped into his chair. Splash settled at his feet, content with his treat. "He seemed to be the guy who'd know what to do with this."

"I'm excited." Mirra smiled again and opened the box. Surprise came first. Then a shivery feeling of happiness. Oh, the man was definitely thinking about her. Nobody would give her a gift like this if he was unaffected by her.

There in the box, nestled against blue silk, was a hammered silver chain with a single stunning pearl. The pearl itself glowed dully against the silk, like the full moon faint in the morning sky.

"Silas. This is breathtaking," Mirra gasped and pulled it from the box.

"Well, it's more from Splash than me." Silas shifted, an uncomfortable look on his face.

"Is that so?" Mirra glanced down at the dog.

"He found it on the beach."

"Did he now? What an intrepid explorer he is."

"Yes, well…" Silas blew out a breath. "I remembered what you said about souls – that they were pearls. And that, well, that I 'owned' yours. So here. You can have it back."

His words came out in a jumbled rush, his lower lip jutting out, a stubborn lift to his chin.

"Ah, I see," Mirra said. And she did – but in a way that she didn't think Silas wanted her to. "You're giving me my soul back."

"Exactly. Everybody's soul is their own. I can't be responsible for yours. I'll…" Silas trailed off.

"You'll what?" Mirra said, the pearl dangling from her hand.

"It's just best you keep it. I can't have the responsibility, you understand?" Silas glowered at her.

"I understand." Mirra stood and turned her back to Silas. "Will you put it on for me?"

"It should just slip –" Silas bit off the words and stood.

Mirra pulled her hair away from her neck and handed him the necklace. Cool hands brushed her neck as he fastened the necklace on, and a shiver went through her at his touch. The pearl slid across her skin, settling at her breasts, and Mirra turned, wanting to touch Silas more than anything in the world. They were inches apart and before he started to move back, Mirra reached up and put a hand to his chest.

His heart rate picked up at her touch, and Mirra smiled. Standing on her tiptoes, she brushed her lips over his.

Silas seemed frozen in place. When he didn't immediately retreat, she slid her hand up his chest and wrapped an arm around his neck, deepening the kiss.

She could tell the minute his control faltered. His hands dove into her hair, pulling her closer, and the world fell away. There was nothing but each other, this moment, the pulse of their souls melding together.

When Irma's voice sounded from the hallway, greeting returning guests, Silas jumped back. A healthy flush tinged his cheeks, and his eyes looked like a hunter's. Mirra shivered, wanting him to continue touching her, wanting to unleash whatever beast lay beneath the control he so carefully wielded.

"This can't happen," Silas said, stepping back from her.

"Why? Because of the cartel?" Mirra suspected it was more, but knew that his pride would prevent him from saying so.

"It's not safe. I'm not safe for you, Mirra. You have to take this seriously."

Mirra touched the pearl at her breasts, and Silas's eyes followed her hands.

"I do take it seriously, Silas. Thank you for my gift."

"It's not a gift. It's just a…a symbol, is all. It's your soul. Not mine. I can't be your protector." Silas backed toward the door, a caged animal ready for flight.

"I understand, Silas. Nevertheless, I thank you for it." Mirra kept her tone light even though her emotions were wound taut.

"You're welcome. And…be careful, okay? Don't just drop by my house anymore. Watch yourself to make sure you aren't being tailed. That kind of stuff. Call me...or call Captain Reid if anything strikes you as weird."

"I don't have your number," Mirra pointed out.

"I'll..." Silas looked wildly around and saw a paper and pen on the counter. He jotted down his number, then all but ran for the door, Splash on his heels.

"I'm glad you came by, Silas," Mirra said as he paused.

"I...right. Thanks for dinner. Tell Irma I said thank you too, please. I have to go now."

"Of course."

Silas was already gone. She heard his truck start up and take off.

Interesting, Mirra thought, rubbing her thumb over the pearl. It felt warm against her skin. If he'd really only wanted to "give her soul back," he could've just handed her the pearl. Instead, he'd taken care with it. He'd sought out Prince, had a necklace made, and had packaged the pearl beautifully. Whether he realized it or not, Silas was already protecting her soul.

Now she just had to figure out how to protect his.

CHAPTER 13

*N*o matter how much he swam, no matter how many push-ups he did, no matter how many times he beat up the old boxing bag in the back of his house, Silas could not banish the memory of kissing Mirra from his brain. It was branded into him, seared to his very soul, and he knew that for the rest of his days he would remember that one perfect moment in her kitchen.

She'd taken him by complete surprise, which was something that was hard to do. But for some reason he hadn't been expecting her response. Already uncomfortable with the delight that had crossed her face when she'd opened the necklace box, Mirra had thrown him completely off when she'd kissed him.

The kiss had been like fire that burned straight through him, rendering him incapable of thought. A wave of longing had washed over him, and for a moment, he'd let it pull him under, let it drag him along for the ride. He'd sunk his hands into her hair and feasted on her mouth.

When he'd surfaced for air, blinking madly at the

vision of beauty before him, it had taken every ounce of Silas's willpower to tear himself away from Mirra. Her eyes saw too much of him. She was the kind of woman who would strip him bare and leave him shivering and vulnerable, curled up in a corner, when she flitted on to the next man.

Or worse – his inability to love would destroy her.

The gift was meant to have been a goodbye gesture, not something to bring them closer together. He didn't want the weight of protecting somebody's soul, even metaphorically speaking. Silas had thought finding the pearl was a perfect way to put an end to Mirra's silly notions about soul gifts and all that. It was about as symbolic as he could get – *here, just take your soul back.* Done and done. Or so he'd thought.

Instead, she'd kissed him and blown his world open, and now, days later, all he could think about was the taste of her.

This couldn't have happened at a worse possible time, Silas thought as he punched the bag once more. Sweat dripped from his body and mosquitos buzzed about him, but Silas paid no mind as he threw another brutal blow at the already beat-up punching bag. He was supposed to be focused on finding out about the cartel.

Not about the soft lips of a beautiful woman.

She was throwing him off his game. Silas threw another punch, and landed a sidekick for good measure. Women would do that to you, he supposed, which was largely why he stayed away from them.

And yet...

There was something about Mirra that called to him.

That made him imagine a different – no, a *better* – future. He'd caught himself on more than one occasion thinking about where he would take Mirra for a picnic. Or wanting to ask her opinion on a chapter he'd just read. It was as though there was an emptiness in his world and she was meant to fill the space.

But Silas had learned as a young boy that dreams were dangerous and hope was for the lucky few.

Checking the dive watch at his wrist, Silas sighed and unwrapped his hands. It was time for him to check in for patrol. Whistling for Splash, who was gnawing on his hunk of rope in the corner of the yard, Silas brought the dog inside to enjoy dinner while he took a cold shower. When his thoughts drifted to Mirra yet again, Silas forcefully shoved them away.

The cartel was close. Captain Reid had received more intel and was being even more diligent about checking in on all of his men. Silas hadn't been the only one to receive a warning, which had led the captain to believe that the cartel had quite a presence on island. Silas wondered why they were using threats instead of trying to buy an officer off. It would have been much easier to bribe their way into having law enforcement look the other way than to scare them off. Most people didn't respond well to threats, especially not testosterone-filled enforcement officers.

Instead of having its intended effect, the knife in the book had only made Silas want to go out and hunt every last cartel member down. Clearly, they didn't know their audience.

The flip side was, maybe they *had* tried to buy off a few officers – maybe they'd even succeeded. If so, that officer was playing the long game and had given no indication of a potential betrayal. Silas considered it – he had to think about every angle – but he trusted Captain Reid's team. He'd picked good men, and he inspired loyalty. In his gut, Silas felt like it would be a tough team to shake.

Toweling off, he steadfastly kept his thoughts on the danger to his life and not the danger to his heart.

"Come on, Splash."

Silas bent and put Splash's vest on. The dog didn't seem to mind wearing it, but Silas had had to be extra careful that he didn't get overheated in the warmer hours of the day. Together, they climbed into Silas's truck and left for the office. The sun had just set, and the sky was tinged the color of blood. He could only hope that wasn't an omen of what was to come.

Now who was being fanciful? It was simply a pretty sunset, not some weird omen of blood on the water.

"Come on," Silas ordered, and Splash hopped down from the truck and followed him into the office.

"Splash!" Captain Reid's face creased with a smile and he bent to pet the dog. "Silas, we need you on the boat ASAP. I'd like you to monitor Lovers' Beach tonight."

"Have you had a tip?"

"There's been more activity. If it's not tonight, it's soon. We need everyone in on this."

"Captain?" Ronaldo – one of Silas's co-workers, and a man he considered a friend – popped his head into the office.

"Hey, man! You're back." Silas greeted Ronaldo with a complicated handshake.

"Yeah, man. The wife finally let me come home,"

Ronaldo said. He'd been on a trip to Colombia to visit his wife's family for the last three weeks. "Captain's brought me up to speed – looks like I got back just in time."

"We certainly could use the help. You'll be on Tortuga Beach tonight," Captain Reid said with a nod to Ronaldo.

"No problem, Captain. Hey, Splash." Ronaldo bent to pet Splash, but the dog didn't come to him; instead he stuck by the captain's legs. "Feeling shy today, buddy?"

"Must sense the tension," Captain Reid said.

"What's to stress about? We've got the intel, now we take these guys down. I'm looking forward to it," Ronaldo laughed.

"These guys are dangerous. I'll expect you to take every precaution."

"We understand." But when Captain Reid looked down at the dog, Ronaldo rolled his eyes at Silas.

"I'll keep Splash here with me tonight. It's best if he's not on the boat," Captain Reid said.

"That makes sense. What's our protocol for backup right now?" Silas asked.

"We're running a bit short. It came down to having coverage on all the beaches with one man per boat, or having a couple of boats with more men on board. I decided to spread it out – it won't take too long for the other boats to show up in case of trouble. We're also working with the police and customs agents. They'll be patrolling by land and water."

"Wow, calling in the big guns, then." Ronaldo laughed again. "I'm excited. We haven't had anything interesting happen here in a while."

"I don't mind boring." Captain Reid leveled a look at

Ronaldo which wiped the smile from the young man's face. "Boring means nobody gets hurt and my island is safe."

"Yes, sir. Of course." Ronaldo shot Silas a sheepish look as they both left the captain's office.

"You have to be careful, man," Silas said as they walked down the dock to their boats. "It sounds like these guys are real trouble."

"What's your plan? How're you gonna handle them?" Ronaldo stopped by his boat and turned to look at Silas.

"Whatever it takes to stop them. At any cost."

"Even your life?"

"I'd prefer to keep my life. But I hate drug runners." Silas shrugged a shoulder. "How many lives could the drugs destroy? If it was pot, I don't know – I'd probably be less inclined to go hard on them. But it sounds like this is the hard stuff. And that's the shit that takes down families. I should know. It killed my mom."

Ronaldo's eyes creased with concern. "Your mother was an addict?"

"Yeah, she was. Died of an overdose right after I was born. Or so I'm told. That's why I've never touched drugs."

"Not even a hit of a jay?" Ronaldo shook his head.

"Nope. Not worth it to me."

"Sorry, man. That's too bad, not having a mama. I can see why you want to take these guys down."

"Just be careful, all right?" Silas said as he boarded his boat.

Ronaldo glanced down at his belt. "I forgot my walkie-talkie. I'm going back in. Stay in touch on the radio tonight."

"I will."

Silas unhooked his lines and motored out onto the water, which had turned a dark grey as the sun had sunk below the horizon. It was calm now, as it often was at sunset, and he let his thoughts wander to what he'd told Ronaldo. It wasn't often that he thought about his mother. Hell, he only had one little snapshot of her tucked away in his wallet. He must have been three months old; she sat on a folding chair in front of their trailer, smiling at the camera, and he was on her lap. The hollows of her cheeks stood out in stark relief. She'd been half in the grave at that point, just one dose away from pushing her heart over the edge. It hadn't been long after that photo that she'd taken her last hit, and to this day Silas wondered if it had been an accident or a choice.

Shaking the thoughts from his head, he slowed to a crawl and turned off his running lights so he could patrol Lovers' Beach. He'd normally never turn his boat lights off at night, but this was not a typical patrol. Settling in, Silas scanned the horizon.

When his radio buzzed, he went to it. "Silas."

"Silas! You have to get back here. Captain's been attacked. They took Splash."

Cold lanced through him. Silas already had the motor on and his boat headed back toward the harbor before he could truly process the words.

Splash was gone.

CHAPTER 14

"*Y*ou can't be here."

Mirra just leveled a look at Silas as he strode to the gate of his garden. It had been days since she'd last seen him, had felt his lips on hers, and she had resisted going to him. But each night as she took to the water and followed the boats, she could feel the danger thickening in the air. Last night, the threat level had spiked, and Mirra had been compelled to seek Silas out this morning.

He looked like hell.

"I understand you want to keep me safe, Silas. But I'm built of stronger stuff than that."

"It doesn't matter what you're built of. You won't stop a bullet," Silas snapped, anger vibrating around him as he stopped at the gate and pushed her hands from the door.

"I can help."

"You *can't* help. You have no idea what we're up against. And you being around is only complicating matters further!" Silas was all but shouting, and Mirra focused on the dark circles around his eyes.

"Why am I complicating things?" Mirra asked, keeping her voice soft.

"Because I think about you all the time and I *can't*. You *can't* be on my mind. I need to stay focused… I…"

When Silas's voice cracked, Mirra ignored his warning and pushed through the gate. She wrapped her arms around his middle, and held on even when he tried to push her hands away. Mirra focused a soothing energy to flow through her and into him, and when Silas began, incrementally, to relax, she eased back slightly and looked up at him.

"I'm your friend, Silas. Won't you tell me what's wrong?"

"They took Splash," Silas whispered.

Mirra froze, her mouth dropping open in shock, and she stepped back to scan the garden for the dog.

"No!" Mirra's shocked gaze flew back to Silas.

He scrubbed a hand over his face and nodded. "I've been up all night, but haven't gotten any further. I…I'm scared for him."

"Silas, can you tell me what happened? What do you know? I can help. I promise you I can help. But you have to talk to me."

"I don't see how you can –" Silas stopped when Mirra held up her hand.

"I've lived here my whole life. I know this island inside and out. I also know almost everyone on island. I can put the word out. People trust me, Silas. They'll help.

We can work together, but I have to know what happened first."

"Why would people help me?" Silas wondered.

"Why wouldn't they? Haven't you helped them?"

"How?"

"You saved my life. I'm certain I'm not the first."

Silas just shrugged and looked over her shoulder, his eyes scanning – constantly scanning.

"Please tell me what happened."

She could see the moment where he gave in, which told her just how scared he was about Splash.

"Come inside, then. I don't like you being out here in the open."

It was the first time he'd invited her into his house – and it was only, Mirra noted, because he felt the need to protect her. Backed him into a corner, that was what she'd done, and she felt zero guilt about it. Nothing mattered now but getting Splash back safely.

Silas led her past the lime tree – part of her mind registered that it looked healthy – and into his house, locking the door behind them. The front door opened directly into a combined living area and kitchen space with two doors that led into what Mirra presumed were the bedroom and the bathroom. The décor was sparse at best. A single armchair sat in front of a small television; a round kitchen table sported two chairs. Notably, the most comfortable thing in the living room was a big squishy bed for Splash in the corner.

"Um, over here." Silas gestured awkwardly to the dining table.

"No couch for you?" Mirra asked.

"No. Why bother? I'm usually in the hammock most nights anyway, to catch the breeze."

"Of course." Mirra desperately wanted to go over to the lone bookshelf across the room and look over its assortment of books and photographs, but now was not the time for idly poking deeper into this man's life. They had a dog to save. "Tell me everything."

"I don't see how —" Silas sighed when Mirra shot him a stern look. "Fine. I went to report for duty last night."

Mirra listened as he gave a quick run-down of their meeting. She held up a hand for a moment to interrupt him. "Was it typical for you to leave Splash behind?"

"Not really, but in these circumstances, it did make sense. His safety is important."

Suspicion niggled in Mirra's gut. "And the captain was certain he'd be safe?"

"Well, obviously there are no guarantees." Silas got up and walked to his coffeepot. He measured out grounds and dumped them in while continuing to talk. "So then they radioed me that the captain got jumped and Splash was gone."

"And where did this happen? They broke into his office?"

"No, the captain had taken Splash out for a walk."

"Why would he do that? That doesn't make sense if he wanted him to be safe, right?" The feeling of suspicion deepened inside Mirra.

"He probably thought Splash had to go potty." Silas shrugged. "Why?"

"How often does Splash really need to go? Like, how long were you out on the boat?"

"Not even an hour, really." Silas narrowed his eyes at her. Leaning back against the counter, he crossed his arms over his chest. "Why? What are you trying to say, Mirra?"

"I'm not trying to say anything. I'm just questioning everything right now. It seems odd to me that if things were really that dangerous... I don't know. I'm just trying to determine why the captain would take Splash for a walk so soon after you left."

"I don't know, Mirra. But I don't like where you're headed with this."

"What did he say happened?"

"He said he was out walking and was jumped from behind. They had Splash and were gone before he could get back up."

"Was he hurt?"

"I think just his pride." Silas held up a coffee cup and Mirra nodded in answer to his silent question.

"So no bruises? Black eyes? Nothing?"

"Not that I could see. Mirra, I really hope you aren't trying to insinuate that the man I consider to be both an impeccable boss and a good friend is behind this." Silas leveled a hard look at her, and she felt her shoulders go up.

"I'm just questioning everything, Silas. I certainly hope it isn't the captain behind this. But don't you think it's smart to ask questions?"

"I think it's smart to find Splash."

"And how are you going to do that if you don't ask questions?"

"It can't be the captain." Silas's voice held enough

warning that Mirra decided to back off and reserve her judgment for later.

"Thank you," she said when he placed the coffee in front of her.

"Um, I don't think I have milk. Sugar?"

"Black is fine. What else do you know?"

"I know that they seem particularly fixated on me. Which is why you can't be showing up here." Silas sat and put his elbows on the table, holding his coffee cup between both hands. He looked so solid and stoic that Mirra wanted to crawl into his lap and kiss his worries away.

"Tell me where you've been and what you've done so far."

"We canvassed the area. I've been to all the beaches. I've searched all night and called for him. Nothing. I don't know what to do," Silas admitted, his eyes aching with sadness.

"Have you posted his photo online? In any of the pet alert groups, that kind of thing?" Mirra asked.

"I'm not on social media."

"Of course you're not." Mirra smiled when Silas's eyes narrowed. "I just meant that I could see where you would find that annoying. Can you send me a picture of Splash? I'll get started getting his photo out. I have very good connections. It'll be faster if we have more eyes on the island looking out for him."

"Why would people look for him, though? They don't know me," Silas said.

"Maybe because despite what you may think, people are innately kind and like to help?"

"That hasn't been my experience."

Mirra's heart cracked for this man who had been shown so little love in his life that he couldn't believe people he didn't know might want to help him find his dog. "It's easy to think the worst of the world, but you'd be surprised at how many people will jump in and try to help. You only have to ask for it."

Silas just shrugged a shoulder and stared off at the wall.

"Okay, enough brooding. Here's what's going to happen. You're going to stop drinking that coffee and lie down for a few hours."

"I can't..." Silas trailed off as Mirra stood and circled the table. Crouching before him, she took his face in her hands.

"Silas. You need to rest. You aren't any help to Splash if you're operating on no sleep. You'll make bad decisions – potentially even one that could hurt him. Send me a picture and let me get on this. Just take a few hours. That's all you need for a refresh. In the meantime, I'll activate the island helpers."

"I don't see –"

"Shh." Mirra silenced him by leaning over to brush the softest of kisses over his lips. It showed exactly how tired he was when his arms came around her and he sank into the kiss for a moment. Oh, this man was crying out for love, Mirra thought.

Pulling away before things could take a different direction and scare him away forever, Mirra met his eyes. "Let me help you, Silas. You have to know how much I care for animals. That's how we met, remember?"

"Foolish woman," Silas mumbled.

"Maybe, but the dolphins are free now, aren't they?"

"Fine. I'll send you his picture."

"Do it now."

"You have to agree to go. I can't sleep if I know you're sitting out here. This isn't a safe place for you, Mirra."

"I'll leave. Right away. But send me his picture first." Mirra waited while Silas drew out his phone and tapped the buttons a few times. She felt her phone vibrate in her pocket and knew he'd sent her the photo.

"I'm setting an alarm on my phone." Silas held up his phone so she could see that he'd set a timer for three hours. "That's all I can take before I go back to looking for Splash."

"I promise that while you sleep, I'll be on the Splash investigation. You aren't letting him down. You're just passing the baton for a moment. You've done everything you can for now. Let someone else handle this while you rest."

Mirra could see how much it pained him to hand over control, but his exhaustion won out.

"Thank you." It might have been gruff, but he meant it.

"That's what friends do, Silas. I'll be in touch."

"I'll walk you to your car."

Mirra almost protested, but knew there was no way he'd let her out into his garden without first scanning for danger. She waited while he stepped outside, her heart hurting for this man who only knew how to tackle problems on his own. Whether he knew it or not, when he'd saved her life Silas had ensured he would never have to walk his path alone again. He'd found himself a family, even if they had to help him from a distance because of the barriers he kept up.

One thing Mirra knew for certain was that she was going to do everything in her power to get this man's dog back.

CHAPTER 15

*M*irra did what anybody did when they wanted the word to get out on island – she went to Prince.

"Well now, it must be my lucky day if a mermaid's showing up at my doorstep." Prince grinned at Mirra from where he sat, a cup of coffee and newspaper in front of him.

"Unfortunately, it's not with good news. Prince, I need your help."

"What's wrong, pretty lady? Come in and tell Prince everything."

Mirra hurried to the little table. "You know Silas, Prince?"

"Sure I do. Dat's a good man." Prince leaned back and crossed his arms over his chest, concern etching the lines of his dark skin.

"Oh right. Duh, you made him my necklace. I love it, by the way." Mirra fingered the pearl at her chest. "Anyway, Silas is in trouble. His dog's been stolen and I need your help in getting the word out. I know you know everyone."

"Naw, not dat cute little Splash? Dat's a good dog right dere."

"I know. And I'm worried he'll be hurt."

"How come he get stolen?"

"It's…to do with his job." Mirra wasn't sure how many details of what Silas had told her she should share.

"Hmm," Prince said, leaning back and kicking his legs out. "Sounds like some bad folks on island right now. I heard tell of dat, I did."

"Did you?"

"Mmhmm." Prince tapped his forehead. "You know dat Prince hear everything."

"Do you know anything I can report to Silas?"

"Nothing yet. But I'll see what I can find out. You got a picture of Splash?"

"I do."

"Send it to me." Prince had already pulled out a sleek iPhone and was tapping at it. For all he enjoyed his disguise of being just a local fisherman, he'd invested in real estate years ago and owned half the island.

"I've sent it. You'll get the word out?"

"I'll let you know soon as I hear something. You and that Silas boy an item?"

"I'd like to be. He's not so sure about it."

"What? Dat man ain't stupid, is he?"

"Doesn't seem to be from what I can tell," Mirra said with a laugh.

"He's a loner."

"Yes, I suspect there's a lot more to his past than he's shared with me."

"He'll come around. Big tree fall hard, and all dat. And you've got yourself a nice axe, child." Prince slapped his knee and laughed.

"We'll see. I hope to make him see that he can rely on people to show up for him. He didn't even know how to ask for help with Splash. Didn't think anyone would want to help him."

"What?" Prince looked shocked. "'Dat's not de island way. We help each other."

"I don't think he's used to asking for it."

"Boy's got a lesson to learn. Go on now, child. I'll be calling you when I have news."

"Thanks, Prince." Mirra stood and pressed a kiss to his cheek, knowing the man was good for his word. She drove home, worry in her heart for Splash.

Later that afternoon, she had just finished filling Irma and Jolie in when her phone rang. They were sitting at the kitchen table, stress-eating chocolate.

"It's Prince." Mirra picked up her phone.

"I hope he has news," Jolie said, cradling her dog, Snowy, in her lap.

"Hi, Prince," Mirra said. "I've got you on speaker with Irma and Jolie."

"Hello, my mermaid beauties. I wish I had better news for you today."

"Oh no, don't tell me he's –" Mirra exclaimed.

"No, de dog is fine. From what I hear, at least."

"That's good news," Mirra murmured, her eyes locking with Irma's.

"Yes. But dey using him as a trap for Silas. Guess dey think he's de biggest threat. Dey take him out and den dey can make de drop. It's big. Like, big big. Dey have no problem killing people."

"But why go to all this trouble? Like to lure him out? Couldn't they just show up at his door or something?"

"I think dey want him on de water. Make it look like an accident."

"Are you saying Splash is on a boat?"

"Yes, dey are holding him on a boat. I guess dey want to lure Silas out and take him out dat way."

Mirra's eyes flew to where the sun was beginning its descent to the horizon. "And they want to do it tonight, don't they?"

"Seems dat way."

"Prince. Can you do me a favor?"

"Anything for you ladies."

"Head Silas off. We're going after Splash."

"Now how am I supposed to stop dat man?"

"Please? You are the cleverest man I know. Figure something out. We'll have Splash back tonight. I can promise you that."

"I don't doubt it. Be careful, ladies. You'd break an old man's heart if you got hurt."

"We will be very careful. We'll follow up with you shortly. Thanks for your help, Prince." It was Irma who spoke then as Mirra was too filled with worry to get her words out.

When Prince hung up, Mirra jumped out of her seat.

"Sit." Irma grabbed Mirra's arm and pulled her back down.

"But we have to go." Panic raced through Mirra.

"And we will go. But with a cool head."

"But –"

"Mirra, give her a chance to speak." Jolie reached out and squeezed her sister's hand.

"If you go and rescue Splash, how will you explain it to Silas after?" Irma's gaze was steady on Mirra's.

"Who cares? He'll be happy Splash is back."

"He's going to want to know how. He's a details guy. You're going to have to have a story."

"I can say a fisherman helped." Mirra shrugged a shoulder. "I can make something up."

"Oh, Mirra." Jolie shook her head. "You know you're a terrible liar."

"That's because I never lie."

"So what makes you think you'll be able to lie now? Especially to him? If you are successful at getting Splash back, you have to understand the ramifications of what might come next." Irma's tone was gentle and her meaning rushed through Mirra.

"I'll have to tell him I'm mermaid." Mirra swallowed past the nerves in her throat.

"You don't have to. But you likely will. Are you prepared for his reaction?"

"He's not going to believe me. I'll have to show him before he believes." Mirra knew Silas would think she was teasing him, and she suspected he wasn't a man who would handle that well.

"He'll either think you're lying or you're crazy," Jolie said.

"The oracle said he was for me and I have to trust

that. If that's the truth, he's going to have to accept me at some point. Unfortunately, it may be before I'm really ready to share with him. Oh, I just wanted more time with him before this came out." Mirra wrung her hands together.

"We don't always get a say in the timing of things," Irma said.

"Give it a chance, Mirra. Look, now you can expect he's going to react poorly. You'll just have to figure out if he's worth it."

"He is." Mirra looked up and met Irma's eyes. "Oh, he needs me. He needs us. He's desperate for love and doesn't even realize it. I have to do this. I have so much love to give."

"You always have," Jolie murmured. "You're the best of us, Mirra. I hope he's worth it, because I'll murder him myself if he hurts you."

"He's going to hurt her, Jolie." Irma looked at her other daughter. "You'll have to let that happen. It's how they'll both learn and grow together."

"Fine. But if it goes on for too long, I reserve the right to feed him to a shark."

"Duly noted," Irma laughed. "Now, shall we plan our attack? The sun is setting and we don't have much time."

The three mermaids put their heads together to figure out how to rescue Splash from the drug lords. Then, plan in place, they stopped by Samantha's house next door to drop Snowy off to play with Pipin.

"You're sure about this?" Mirra asked Jolie once more as they neared the water line.

"I've been enticing men for years now. This will be no

problem." Jolie laughed and tossed her dark hair over her shoulders.

"Yeah, but you're with Ted now. He may not like it."

"I think, given the circumstances, he'll understand. My intention is pure."

"Okay then. Let's rescue Splash."

Together the women walked into the water, having shed their clothes on the sand, and they all dove deep, changing effortlessly into their mermaid forms. For a long time, their magick had worked best only during the full moon. But over the years, they'd been gifted with more strength, particularly because Irma's father had felt so horribly for his daughter on the loss of her love.

The mermaids called to the dolphins, knowing their friends would have seen all activity around the island. When the pod surrounded them moments later, they followed the dolphins easily until they'd found the boat Splash was on.

The women formed a circle in the depths below the boat and held hands for a moment before splitting up. Jolie and Irma swam to the front of the boat, where they would provide distraction. Mirra had the most dangerous part – to get close to the back of the boat so Splash would come to her. She wouldn't be able to dive deep with him, so she'd need to rescue the dog and surface-swim with him as fast as she could before anyone on the boat realized he was gone.

Mirra surfaced silently at the back of the boat. She heard the chatter of men and the shout when someone spotted Jolie. It didn't take long to hear the running of feet as Jolie began to sing – a song that no man could resist.

Certain that she was safe, Mirra pulled herself up to the platform at the back of the boat.

"Splash!" Mirra whispered, spying the dog tied to a rung of a bench. The dog jumped up and shook with joy when he saw her. Judging the distance, Mirra decided to stay in her mermaid form. Brandishing her knife, she hopped forward and easily cut the rope restraining Splash. The dog licked her face ecstatically.

"Come on, buddy, you'll have to trust me."

Mirra inched back until she could slide her tail into the water, and before she could even turn and hold her hands up to the dog, Splash had jumped into the water next to her with a resounding, well, splash. It was clear where the dog had gotten his name, Mirra thought, as she scooped him into her arms.

Turning on her back so that the dog rested on her chest with his snout out of the water, she propelled herself from the boat, her heart racing. All the while, Jolie entranced the men at the front of the boat.

When Mirra deemed herself far enough away, she threw her head back and bellowed to the stars – her signal for Jolie and Irma to dive deep and disappear. The shouts rang out, but Mirra was too far away for anyone on the boat to spy her.

"You're okay now, buddy. I got you," Mirra repeated over and over while Splash continued to swipe his tongue across her face.

They soon neared her beach, close enough that Mirra knew Splash could swim to shore. Changing back into her human form, she bounded out after the dog and grabbed the sarong she'd left for herself. Winding it around her body, she dropped to her knees to give Splash a proper cuddle and waited for Irma and Jolie to appear. When the minutes drew out, Mirra's heart began to race.

"Don't worry! We just stopped to help a turtle stuck in some fishing line." Jolie's head popped up from the water.

"Thank goodness! I was beginning to think they'd come after you."

"Nah, we were way too fast. By the time they came out of our spell, we were far gone. Is he okay?" Jolie dropped to her knees in the sand to pet a very happy dog.

"Seems to be. I don't see any cuts on him or anything, and he's not limping. I think Prince was right. They weren't hurting him – they were using him for bait."

"Poor doggo. You deserve steak, don't you?" Irma bent over and pet Splash.

"I have to call Silas. I just…"

"You're worried what he'll say."

"There's more. I saw one of the men's shirts. It was a Marine Enforcement shirt."

"No." Jolie's eyes widened. "Did you see who it was?"

"I just caught a flash of the sleeve before I ducked back into the water."

"There's a traitor on board."

Mirra nodded and hugged Splash to her, only hoping that Silas wouldn't think she was in on it too.

CHAPTER 16

*A*fter Splash had been appropriately cooed over and fed some choice bits of steak, Mirra changed into a flowing pink dress and braided her hair back from her temples. Finally, she called Silas.

"I have Splash," Mirra said, cutting off Silas's hello.

"What! Oh my god, is he okay?"

"He's just fine. We've spoiled him with a bit of steak and he's enjoying basking in our adoration."

"I'm on my way."

Mirra held out the phone and looked at it, and then put it down. Walking into the garden, she dropped onto a lounge chair and patted the cushion so Splash would join her. Irma and Jolie had wisely disappeared, so all she could do now was wait. Rubbing the pearl on her necklace between her fingers, Mirra worried over the impending conversation she would have to have with Silas.

It wasn't long before she heard a truck door slam outside. Knowing Irma would let Silas in, Mirra waited where she was. With that unknown connection dogs have with their owners, Splash had perked up and was standing at the end of the lounge chair. When Silas rounded the corner into the garden, he took off like a shot and beelined to his owner.

"Splash!" Silas dropped to his knees in the sand and wrapped his arms around the wiggling dog, who bathed his face in licks. Laughing, Silas pulled back and ran his hands over the dog's coat, looking for any sign of injury.

"I couldn't find any marks on him. He seems fine."

"Mirra." Still kneeling in the sand, Silas looked up at her, and the look in his eyes almost took her breath away. She'd given him back a piece of himself, and she didn't want that gratitude to go away when he heard her story. Gnawing at her lip, Mirra crossed her arms across her stomach.

"I know. I was just as happy to see he was safe," Mirra murmured.

Standing, Silas walked to the lounge chair next to hers and Splash followed, jumping up on the cushion and crawling into Silas's lap when he sat. "Is it okay that he's on the cushions?"

"Of course. I think he needs to be close to you right now." *And so do I*, Mirra added silently. Every time she was near Silas it was like her heart did a little dance inside her chest. Never having thought she could be envious of a dog, Mirra now looked begrudgingly at Splash reclining across Silas's lap.

"How did you get him back? Where did you find him?" An actual smile creased Silas's face, and Mirra's stomach turned. She wasn't ready to ruin this feeling yet.

"Well," Mirra demurred, "I went to Prince – as you do

when you need to get the word out on this island. He said he likes you."

"Did he? I like Prince. I play dominoes with him from time to time."

"He'll fleece you, too. Don't bet money." Mirra laughed.

"I learned that after two games." Silas cracked another smile and Mirra let out a little sigh. Two smiles in the space of a few minutes was unheard of for Silas.

"Smart of you. Well, Prince said he'd heard some chatter about some bad dudes on island and promised to ask around. It took him about an hour to find Splash."

"Prince found him? I'll have to stop by and thank him." Silas squeezed Splash.

"Well, Prince located him. It was actually the three of us who rescued him." Mirra pointed to the villa and made a little circle with her finger.

"*You* rescued him? That sounds dangerous, Mirra. You should have called me and let me handle it."

"From my understanding, that was exactly what they wanted."

"How so?" Silas squinted at her.

"Prince said they were using Splash as bait. They wanted to get you out to look for him, and then they could get rid of you. As in…you know, *get rid of* you. Murder," Mirra clarified when Silas still seemed puzzled.

"That seems…excessive. Why in the world would they do that?" Silas's brow furrowed.

"I honestly don't know. I said the same."

"I feel like most drug runners want to keep as low a profile as possible. Get in, get out. Make the drop. Get the money. That kind of thing. At least that's been my experience. Why on earth would they risk screwing that all up by trying to murder a marine park agent? It sounds like it would just complicate things."

"I can't say. I don't really know how criminals think." Mirra thought about the flash of the Marine Enforcement uniform she had seen and wondered if she should tell Silas outright, or perhaps suggest that someone was betraying him. She bounced the thought around, then looked up when Silas tapped her leg. "Sorry, I was just wondering whether...whether there's something more involved going on here."

"I can't say until you tell me the rest of the story." Silas looked at her patiently. She lost herself for a moment, wanting to crawl into his lap and have him tell her that everything would be okay for them in the future. Knowing that was impossible, Mirra sighed.

"So, Splash was being kept on a boat off the eastern coast. They were going to lure you out somehow and make your death look like an accident."

"How do you know that?"

"That's what Prince told me." Mirra shrugged and toyed with the pearl at her neck. "I tend to trust what he says."

"I'm going to have to find out who Prince has been talking to."

"Good luck," Mirra laughed. "He wouldn't be the guy who knows everything on island if he told people where he heard things."

"That's a good point. Okay, so Splash is on the boat – oh my god, Mirra, please tell me you didn't swim to the boat like the dolphins." Silas's eyes widened, and he bent over and gripped her knee. "Please do not tell me that you took this on by yourself."

"Well, it was the three of us."

"Mirra. There's no way you could have swum past those men. I know you're a strong swimmer, but that is just…" Silas shook his head in disbelief. For a moment, Mirra considered going along with the story he'd given her. It would make her seem foolish, but it wouldn't reveal to him who and what she really was.

"And if I did swim to the boat?" Mirra asked softly, searching Silas's face.

"That's…it could take you hours to get there if they were far offshore. Did you use a friend's boat? How?"

Again, another out she could take. Sighing, Mirra shook her head. "I have to tell you two things, both of which I need you to listen to with an open mind before you react."

"Sure." Silas raised an eyebrow at her.

"You have to *promise* you'll listen with an open mind."

"I promise. I will."

"First one is…I think someone in your unit is betraying you."

Shock rippled across Silas's face, followed by anger. "If this is you trying to tell me the captain is a traitor, you can forget it. I trust that man with my life."

"I'm not saying it's the captain. I don't know who it is. But…" Mirra held up her hands.

"Why do you think this?"

"Because I saw someone wearing a Marine Enforcement uniform on the drug runners' boat."

Silence greeted her statement, and Mirra waited it out, her heart hammering in her chest.

"You're certain?"

"Yes. I'm sorry, Silas."

Silas pinched the bridge of his nose and sighed. Sensing his distress, Splash picked his snout up and licked Silas's chin. Absentmindedly, Silas began to stroke Splash's fur. "Let's just think about this for a second before we go slinging accusations around –"

"It would make more sense why they stole Splash and tried to lure you out," Mirra pointed out. "That seems more personal to me. You said you thought it was too elaborate for a drug lord to get involved in such a ploy, and I agree."

"But I don't know anybody who'd have anything against me," Silas said, his eyes taking on a wounded look.

"It might not have anything to do with you personally. Maybe they just think you're the biggest obstacle in their way. Are you cool with all your co-workers??"

"I thought we were all solid. I occasionally meet a few for beers. We play a pick-up game of ball every once in a while. It's a tight-knit group."

"And the captain?" Mirra winced when Silas shot her a glare.

"Why do you keep zeroing in on him?"

"I'm just asking questions. Remember, I don't know these people or your relationship with them. I'm trying to understand. And, with the captain, it just seemed odd that someone could so easily overcome him and steal Splash."

"He gets disoriented easily."

"What?"

"He lost his sight in his left eye. It's why he mans the

desk now. He could be jumped pretty easily. In fact, he loses his balance here and there because of it."

"Ah," Mirra said. "So if someone knew that about him…"

"Damn it," Silas swore. When Splash stiffened in his lap, he automatically cradled the dog closer to soothe him. "You're right. Anyone who knows that about the captain could have surprised him easily."

"I know you don't want it to be someone at the Marine Enforcement. I'm sorry," Mirra said.

"I really don't want it to be. I just can't… I can't wrap my head around this."

"Maybe someone's hard up. Money can be a strong motivator if there's a lot of debt. Or a family sickness, that kind of thing." Mirra shrugged.

"I need to think about this for a moment." Silas looked up and met her eyes dead on. "You might as well go on with the second thing you were going to tell me."

"Right, about that." Mirra shifted nervously. "I…I really need you to stay open-minded here, remember? But you're asking for an explanation of how we rescued Splash and, well, I can't lie to you."

"I wouldn't expect you to lie to me."

"But, because of that, I have to share a secret with you that very few people know. I'm counting on you to respect that."

"Of course." Silas tilted his head at her in question. "I'm very good at keeping secrets. I don't like most people anyway, and trust even fewer."

"Right. So, what do you know about the history of Siren Island?"

Silas just looked at her, as if she were a dotty old woman nattering on about some story or another. "Like how it was colonized?"

"More like…how it got its name?"

"Ah, right. The mermaid myth. The mermaid and her lover. He died. She watches over the reef. The soul thing." Silas nodded to the pearl she worried between her fingers.

"Right. That. So…" Mirra took a deep breath. "That story is actually true."

Silas laughed. "Right, and you can call me Poseidon."

"I'm serious, Silas. That's…those are my people. I'm a mermaid."

Silas entire body went still, and he held her eyes. "You're serious?"

"Yes, very serious." Mirra rushed on when he said nothing, "It's how we got to the boat so quickly. We were able to change into our mermaid forms and communicate with the dolphins. They led us to the boat. Jolie – well, she's good at enticing men, so we used her as a distraction while I climbed onto the boat and cut Splash loose. I carried him on my chest and swam at the surface back to the beach."

"You…" Silas's mouth gaped open.

"I know it's a lot to take in, but I promise I'm not lying to you."

"The dolphins?" For a moment, Mirra thought Silas might actually believe her. She remembered how the dolphins had helped him carry her back to his boat when she'd been injured.

"They helped. Yes. Just like they helped you rescue me," Mirra whispered, searching his face for any sign of acceptance. When she saw the harsh look come into his eyes, Mirra closed hers to hold back the tears that welled.

"I don't know what you're playing at, Mirra, but this is no game." Silas stood, Splash in his arms, his voice rising. "It's not fair of you to make up this nonsense. To take up my time with this…bullshit. I refuse to believe this."

"Silas, I'm not lying to you," Mirra said, keeping her voice soft, meeting his eyes.

"You expect me to believe that my Captain, someone I work with, day in and day out – someone I trust with my life – has betrayed me, and then I'm supposed to just swallow your mermaid story like it's no big deal? I think the only thing more ridiculous than your story is that you actually thought I might believe this crap. In fact, isn't it convenient that *you're* the one who found Splash? I don't really know you, Mirra, but I certainly know the men I work with. And I'm finding it increasingly concerning that you have all these details about where Splash was and who was on the boat – and then you try to pass it off with some dumb story of being a mermaid? Nice try, sugar. I'm not that stupid."

"Silas. Please, you have to believe me." Mirra stood and reached for him, but he stepped back, confusion in his eyes. "I don't want you to get hurt. I –"

"You what, Mirra?"

She couldn't tell him she loved him. Not when he was looking at her like she was a witch he wanted to burn at the stake.

"I care for you, Silas. I'm scared you're going to get seriously hurt."

"I've lasted this long on my own just fine, sugar. I'll

ask you stay the hell out of my way. Thanks for not hurting Splash."

"As if I would hurt a dog!" Mirra gasped, bringing her hand to her chest, truly wounded.

"Maybe not. But all of this is just too convenient for me. Stay away from me. I mean it this time. I want nothing to do with your lies. If I find out you're anywhere near our boats, I'll have you locked up myself."

With that, Silas stormed from the garden, Splash turning in his arms to stare mournfully after her.

She'd known it was going to be bad. But she hadn't known it would tear her heart in two.

Irma slipped from the shadows and took Mirra by the shoulders, guiding her into the house to do what mothers had done for centuries – patch up broken hearts.

CHAPTER 17

Splash whined in Silas's arms, and he bent to press a kiss to his dog's head.

"It's okay, buddy. You're safe now."

The dog struggled against his hold and Silas adjusted his grip, making sure not to squeeze him too tightly, as a whirlwind of emotions overtook him.

She'd looked like a virgin sacrifice.

Ethereal in her light pink gown, her blond hair flowing down her back and her eyes luminous in her face – Mirra had overwhelmed him. He'd almost forgotten himself for a moment, wanting so desperately to go to her – to lay his head in her lap and have her wrap her arms around him and tell him everything was going to be okay.

Instead, she'd fed him a lie, and his entire image of her had shattered.

"Here you go, boy." He deposited Splash in the front seat of his truck – then the dog did something Silas had never seen him do before.

He threw his head back and howled.

"Splash!" Silas reached out to grab the dog's collar to keep him from jumping back out of the truck. "What is *with* you right now?"

"He doesn't want to go."

Silas turned, his shoulders tensed, and met Irma's gaze. She leaned against the post that held the Laughing Mermaid sign. A flowing sarong in deepening shades of turquoise was wrapped around her body, and her eyes were steady on his. In this moment, Silas could almost believe they *were* mermaids. The very essence in which these women carried themselves was sensuous almost to the point of overconfidence. Fluidly strong, beautiful, and almost otherworldly. These women might not actually be mermaids, but they were still from a different world than his.

"I find that hard to believe. He loves me."

"We saved him. He understands what that means." Irma's words stung Silas.

"Oh, what? You're saying you own his soul now?"

"I'm saying he knows he is loved here."

"*I* love him. He's my best friend." Silas was surprised to hear his voice break. Anger rolled in his stomach. He was furious that Splash had been stolen, furious that Mirra was lying to him, and furious that there might be a traitor on his team. Ready for battle, he raised his chin at Irma.

"Stand down, soldier." Irma smiled, reading his emotions correctly. "Your quarrels aren't with me."

"I need to go," Silas bit out.

"You shouldn't drive when you're this upset."

"I'll manage."

"Silas. Will you turn your back on her?"

"I have to. She's either lying or delusional."

Disappointment crossed Irma's face and there was something about her expression that hit him in a way he didn't know how to respond to. If she had yelled at him, he would have known how to handle that.

"I expected more from you." Though Irma's words were soft, they might as well have been a knife to his gut.

"You can't...possibly think..." Silas trailed off as Irma stared coolly at him. His gaze flew up to the Laughing Mermaid sign above her head, then back to her, all but glowing in the moonlight. For a moment, confusion warred with anger in his gut.

"I don't need to think. I know."

Silas shook his head to clear the fog that seemed to crowd it. Too many emotions, too many untruths – it was all making him feel like he was living in an upside-down world. What he needed right now was laser-like focus, because he knew he had a target on his back.

He rounded the truck, saying, "I have to go."

"Run away, Silas. It's what you're good at, I presume?"

Caught, Silas stopped and looked at her. "Sometimes you have to run away to save yourself."

"And you see Mirra as a threat?"

Silas couldn't think of an answer that wouldn't insult Irma or Mirra, or reveal too much of who he was. Instead, he just shook his head and climbed into the truck.

As he drove away, he tried not to think about what he was leaving behind. Because Irma was right – Mirra *was* a threat to him. Thoughts of her distracted him through the day. Her presence in his garden disrupted his routine.

Much like the lime tree she'd given him, Mirra needed tending, nurturing – hell, even love.

And he was not in the position to give that to anyone. He'd spent his whole life scrambling to finally find a spot where he could feel safe and content, could have a general sense of well-being about life. Splash was the first thing he'd ever let into his life that required care from him, and he'd already screwed that up by letting him get stolen. Taking on a beautiful woman with delusions of being a mermaid? Not happening.

"I'm sorry, buddy." Silas reached out and petted Splash's soft ears while the dog continued to whine as they drove into town. "I let you down. I should've kept you with me at all times."

Silas pulled the truck to a stop in front of Prince's house, hoping the man would be around. He had questions that he hoped Prince would have answers for. Picking up Splash, Silas scanned the area before stepping to the garden wall.

"You've got him!" Prince shouted from across the garden, where he stood under a palm tree with a long-handled saw in his hands. Silas waited as he finished sawing and three coconuts plopped to the ground with heavy thuds. "Come in, come in."

"Thanks," Silas said and opened the gate. Bending down, he put Splash on the ground and the dog immediately ran over to greet Prince, who lavished him with praise.

"Dat's a fine warrior, he is," Prince said, stroking Splash's ears.

"He's safe. Doesn't seem to be hurt at all. I'm told you were the one who was able to track him down."

"Sho and I heard some things." Prince picked up a coconut and held it in the air as an offer to Silas.

"No, thank you."

"Splash, you go by your dad for a moment." Prince picked up his machete and, when he was certain the dog was clear, brought it down on the coconut in a sharp movement. In moments, he had split the coconut and was wandering across the garden with his drink. "Come, boy. Sit with an old man."

"I really can't stay long. I need to report to the captain."

"He'll hold. Dis is important."

"Can you tell me what you heard?" Silas asked, taking the rickety chair across from Prince. Splash settled at his feet, and Silas couldn't begin to describe how much he'd missed having the dog at his feet. His little shadow, he thought.

"Dese some bad dudes," Prince said. He took a sip from his coconut and stretched his legs out in front of him. Shaking his head back and forth, he pursed his lips. "You need to be careful."

"I'm trying to be. But I don't know who to trust."

"You can trust me."

"Can I? You *were* the one with the information, after all." Silas held Prince's eyes.

"Well, dat's because people talk to me. You know why people talk to me? Because dey trust me. I can keep secrets."

"But you betrayed someone's trust to tell Mirra where Splash was."

"I didn't. Mirra don't know where I heard dat from. Plus, comes a time a man has to make a choice."

"And what's that?"

"I like my island, Silas." Prince took another swig of coconut juice. "I like dat it's peaceful. We can leave our doors open here. I don't like when people come in and throw money around. Flashy folks. Dey trying to make trouble. We're not dat kind of island. So I make choices."

"You choose to operate for the greater good."

"I like peace, man. Keep it easy. Keep it friendly. Dese dudes? Dey not from around here. I don't like it. But not everyone feels dat way. Some people, well, dey need de money, you know?"

"I understand what it is to be poor, Prince."

"Do you?" Prince's dark eyes creased at the corners as he assessed Silas.

"I understand hunger so painful you double over with it, to the point where you go numb and stop feeling hungry at all. I understand always looking over your shoulder and carrying everything you own in a backpack. I understand being faced with tough choices. But there's one thing different between me and them."

"What's dat?"

"I chose to find a way. One that didn't involve hurting other people."

"You got de smarts boy, dat's why. Not everyone got dat." Prince tapped the shock of white hair sticking up from his head. "You get yourself an education?"

"The streets taught me what I need to know."

"Ah, but you could read when you hit de streets? Or you learn on de way?"

"I could read."

"Some of dese boys can't. Dey don't know any better. We try to help where we can."

Silas assumed that by "we" he meant the island people. "But some of them just want the money."

"Right on. Some of dem…well, dey blinded by de money. I seen it before, too. Dey get a whole load of money fast, and dey spend it even faster. No concept of saving. No money management skills. At de end of de day…dey not much better off for it anyway."

"I've seen the same. Prince, can you give me anything to go on?"

"Watch your back, man. Watch your back. You can trust me. You can trust de mermaids. But everybody else, you think twice, you hear me?"

Silas stilled. "What do you mean, 'the mermaids'? You mean the women at the Laughing Mermaid? Mirra and the others?"

"Yes, dey solid."

"Right. Solid." Silas blew out a breath and crossed his arms over his chest. He stayed silent as all those icky emotions warred in his gut.

"You like her?"

"Who?"

"Don't be playing with me, man." Prince slapped his thigh and laughed. "Mirra came running to me as soon as she heard Splash was gone."

"She's very nice."

"More than nice. She's de most amazing woman I

know aside from my Maria. Well, now, dat's not fair. Most women are de best I know," Prince rocked back with another laugh and slapped his knee. "But Mirra? She's a special one."

"Is she? How so?"

"I think you know." Prince leveled a look at him.

"I don't think I really do, Prince. Because if you're saying what I think you're saying, then I'd have to question your sanity." Silas lifted his chin, challenging the man.

"Oh, I see, I see." Prince rocked back and forth, chuckling. "And de man calls himself a sailor."

"I *am* a sailor."

"Man, you got a mermaid tattooed on your own arm." Prince continued to laugh. "But you telling me you don't believe?"

"It's not..." Silas's words dried up as he looked down at his arm and back to Prince. "It's not what I believe, Prince. It's just a fact. Like...the sky is blue. It's not red."

"Sometimes de sky is red. You seen a sunset or two where it all goes red."

"That's the sun's rays. The color of the sky doesn't go red."

"Sure it do. And at night it goes dark. De point is... dere's shades to everything. Not all black and white. Right or wrong, yes or no."

"Prince. Listen. You have to level with me. Are you telling me straight up that you believe in mermaids?"

"Of course." Prince delivered his answer so simply that Silas paused for a moment and took a deep breath. Was the world around him just going mad collectively?"

"Prince. You can't..." Silas ran a hand over his face, fatigue settling in. "It's just..."

"People can believe what dey want. I'm not trying to tell you what to think."

"But...it's just...they're mythical creatures, is all. The stuff of legends. I don't think it's fair – or kind, really – to perpetuate a myth. To..." Silas gestured with his hand in the air. "To feed into someone's delusions like that. It's more harmful to build those up instead of trying to help someone see reason. To see the real world."

Prince looked at him for a long moment, then his eyes widened. "You tink dey crazy? Is dat it?" Prince roared with laughter. "Oh, I'm surprised Irma didn't lay you out. She's de most levelheaded woman I know."

"That is the impression I originally got, yes."

"I'm surprised you're still standing. She's a scary woman, dat Irma. I love her to pieces. Don't tell my Maria dat."

"She said she was disappointed in me," Silas admitted, absentmindedly rubbing a hand over his chest.

"Ah, stings when dey do dat, don't it?" Prince nodded. "It's like your momma scolding you."

"I wouldn't know," Silas said absently, his mind else-where as he tried to come to terms with the fact that mermaids might be real. Was this something islanders did to punk people? He missed the look of concern that briefly crossed Prince's face at his words.

"You don't got no momma?"

"I don't have anyone, Prince. Except for Splash." Silas rose.

"A smart man don't turn his back on de offer of family."

"Nobody's offered me family."

"Did Mirra tell you what she was?"

"She told me what she *thinks* she is."

"Den she offered you family. You'd better tink twice about what you're walking away from, man."

CHAPTER 18

"*P*atience. All she needs is just a little patience…" Jolie sang sweetly.

Mirra threw a tortilla chip at her. They were sitting out in the garden beneath the stars. It was the next night, and Jolie had decided that Mirra had moped around long enough. She'd come out with a pitcher of margaritas and a tower of nachos.

Mirra sniffed. "I don't think this has anything to do with patience."

"I believe there was a time, not too long ago…let's see…" Jolie pursed her lips. "Right, right – it was when I was mooning after Ted. And you kept telling me to just be patient. And even though it killed me, I was patient."

"Were you? I can't seem to recall that." Mirra sniffed again and took a sip of her margarita.

"Well, as patient as someone like me can be."

"This isn't about patience," Mirra insisted. "It's something more than that. He doesn't trust me, you see? He doesn't really trust anyone. Which I could try to understand if he'd open up to me more, but I can barely have a conversation with him. He shoves me away as soon as he starts to relax around me."

"Right. Got it. Men are scum."

"Jolie…" Mirra shook her head.

"The absolute worst. Only good to scratch an itch with, and toss away when you're finished with them. Really, I think you're better off here." Jolie kicked back on the lounger and dipped a chip in some salsa like she didn't have a care in the world.

Irritation worked through Mirra. Of course *Jolie* didn't have anything to worry about. Her partner, Ted, loved her and treated her like the goddess she was.

"Silas isn't the worst. He's just…"

"A jerk?" Jolie offered.

"No. He's wounded."

"Isn't everyone, in some way or another? We've all had troubles."

"Not like this, Jolie. I'd say we've led a pretty charmed life."

"Well, yeah, but we're not fully human either, so there's that. But keep in mind – we also didn't have a father figure growing up. We could have had all sorts of daddy issues."

"We could've. But I'd say we've turned out pretty well, don't you think?"

"I think we're fantastic." Jolie laughed. Turning, she looked at Mirra. "But you might find a common thread there. If he really did struggle growing up, I suspect it's likely he has issues about his parents."

"He said he took off when he was young."

"So he knows about not having parental figures. You could maybe find some common ground there?"

"It's a stretch. I don't think anyone could look at our mother and think that we were lacking for love. She'd mother the whole world if she could."

"That's true, isn't it? We certainly lucked out there."

"I just… I want to go to him. But I can't. I just can't," Mirra repeated. She took another sip of her drink, letting the tang of the lime flow across her tongue. "It's like… what, I'm going to be the heartsick girl who keeps throwing herself at his doormat? Like, how desperate do I have to be?"

"I agree that it isn't in our nature to throw ourselves at men. But maybe you just need to wait a bit, until this whole drug thing is over? Because it also sounds like he's genuinely worried for your safety. You scare him every time you show up at his door, because he's looking over your shoulder for someone to come after you. And it's only going to be worse now that they went after Splash too. He might just not be in the place to even think about, let alone receive, love."

"Since when did you get so smart?" Mirra narrowed her eyes at Jolie.

"I've always been smart. It's just that you were blinded by my beauty for all these years."

"Did I say smart? I meant annoying."

"Also that. I consider it part of my charm."

"I can't imagine how Ted puts up with you."

"Probably because of that whole 'blinding people with my beauty' thing." Jolie shot her such a wide shit-eating grin that Mirra had to laugh.

"You're a pain in the butt."

"But I'm *your* pain in the butt. Seriously though, Mirra, I'm worried about you with all this. Your heart has always been so big. I hate seeing you in pain. I can't believe Silas doesn't see what is right in front of him."

"You can't expect everyone to just accept mermaids."

"I don't! But the man has a freaking mermaid tattooed on his arm. I mean, come on! You'd think he'd be somewhat open-minded."

"Maybe being open-minded is a privilege."

"Oh sure, now you want to get deep on me?" Jolie reached for another chip.

"I just mean..." Mirra leaned back and thought for a moment, her eyes on the stars, the breeze rustling the palm leaves above. "If you've had to make your own way your whole life...had to fight for everything you have...maybe you don't get the luxury of being open-minded. Maybe you have to deal in absolutes."

"I guess. I can't profess to know what that's like."

"I just know...like, *I know*..." Mirra held her fist to her core. "...that Silas is the one for me. And I think he senses it too. I can see it in his eyes. But I have to figure out a way past his walls."

"Patience."

"I'm going to punch you," Mirra decided.

"My vote is you ride out the drug lord situation. Because Silas is right – it is serious. It *is* scary. And these are bad dudes. You could feel the energy around their boat when we were there. They'll shoot first and ask questions later."

"And I'm just supposed to sit back and let him get shot at?"

"I didn't say that. But you can monitor him from afar. When the threat has passed and things are normal again – go to him and show him who you are."

"I just want… I want him to – for a moment, just a moment – to *see* me without me having to bash him over the head with what we are. I want him to give a little."

"Maybe he's already given as much as he can."

"It doesn't feel like much." Mirra took another swig of her margarita.

"That's because you're someone who's open and comfortable with her emotions. Silas is clearly extremely guarded. You don't know what's brought him to that point. For all you know, he may think he's bared his soul to you."

"Great. Just great. Of course I have to end up with the emotionally stunted man."

"Not emotionally stunted." Jolie sat up and reached for Mirra's arm. "That's not a fair assessment of someone who's been hurt. He may feel all the feels. His emotions may be so huge that the only thing he knows how to do is keep them locked down. Some people feel so deeply that it's like a wave crashing over them. Don't dismiss him just because he doesn't communicate or process emotions the same way you do."

"You think he feels a lot for me?"

"I think you're scaring the ever-loving shit out of him. And that's a good thing. It's okay to rock the boat if your intentions are pure. You're a threat to his carefully crafted lifestyle. Give him time."

"He hurt me," Mirra said.

"And he'll likely hurt you again. Love isn't always pretty. You just have to decide if the hurt is too great for you to see past his defense mechanisms and still love him."

"I don't have a choice, do I? The oracle said he's for me."

"The oracle also says you always have free will. You can change directions any time you want to. She doesn't deal in absolutes."

"She has a pretty good track record so far."

At that Jolie laughed and tossed her hair over her shoulder. "She does. Speaking of which, I'm going to go find my absolute and give him some love."

"Sure, rub it in."

"Naturally. You won't be far behind. Don't give up on Silas, Mirra. I get the feeling that everyone else in his life has."

"I won't. I can't." Mirra lifted her face to accept her sister's kiss on the cheek, and then let her mind drift as she stared up at the stars. Finally, she sighed and stood up, stretching her arms above her head and working the kinks from her shoulders.

She'd already known she would go to him tonight. There was no way Mirra was going to leave Silas alone to defend himself against this cartel.

After slipping her loose dress over her head, Mirra wandered naked to the water, the breeze lightly kissing her skin. The water churned around her legs, welcoming her back home, and Mirra dove into the next oncoming wave. Her magick flowed over her, as much a part of her as her eye color, and in moments she'd transformed to mermaid.

Mirra took her time tonight, swimming her usual circuit to check the reefs and assess any recent damages. The ocean at night was a different entity, one where the little guys came out to play, the turtles found nests to sleep, and bioluminescence danced on the waves. Usually, the rhythms of the water soothed Mirra, but tonight she couldn't relax. Danger was imminent, and she felt helpless to change its course.

When she surfaced, Mirra was far enough from Silas's boat that she was certain he couldn't see her. She'd stay here for hours, until he brought the boat home and she was positive he was safe.

For once, Silas would have someone watching his back, even if he didn't know about it.

CHAPTER 19

*M*irra slept late the next day. Silas had been on his boat clear through the night until dawn, and she'd stayed with him every minute of it. She couldn't decide whether she was happy that there had been no danger or even more on edge than before. It felt like they were in a holding pattern, and Mirra found she really didn't enjoy the feeling of being out of control. Her sleep had been riddled with fitful dreams and when she finally got up, it felt like she hadn't rested at all.

"I was wondering when we were going to see you." Irma sat at the kitchen table, typing quickly on her rose-gold laptop, a cup of tea in front of her.

"I didn't come in until sunrise."

"Give me one second to finish this. It's an email to a guest."

Mirra made herself a cup of tea and popped an English muffin in the toaster oven. While she waited, she did some stretches to work out the ache in her neck. The sun was already beginning its descent toward the water, which meant Mirra only had a couple more hours before she would be back in the ocean to shadow Silas for another night. She wasn't sure what help she was going to provide when the time came, but when push came to shove, Mirra could harness her magick to make a powerful impact if need be.

"Now, tell me. How did last night go?" Irma closed her laptop and turned her eyes to her daughter.

"It was quiet." Mirra shrugged a shoulder and pulled a pot of strawberry jam from the refrigerator. "I stayed with him all night, but nothing to report."

"No intel from our water friends?"

"Same stuff. Something bad is coming but we don't know when."

"That's frustrating."

"It is. I want this to be over. I feel like I could move forward with Silas, but we can't so long as this is hanging over our heads."

"Mirra…it's always going to be something, though." Irma's face creased in concern. "That's the danger of falling for someone who has a job like he does. You're going to have to accept that this may not be the only time you pull an all-nighter or stay up worrying for him."

"But…" Mirra hadn't really considered the possibility that this could happen again down the road. She'd just thought they had to conquer this particular battle. Kind of like a video game – beat the big bad guy and they'd win. She hadn't thought about there being another bad guy over the horizon. "Oh. I didn't think about that."

"It's not like Siren Island is a popular spot for drug trafficking or anything like that. But Silas does have a somewhat dangerous job. Are you prepared to accept that? Because I don't suspect he'll up and leave his job anytime soon. You may *always* be worrying about him."

"I…wow, I didn't think past the immediate future. But you're right. And I can't ever expect him to leave a career he finds fulfilling." Mirra pursed her lips as she thought more deeply about what her future with Silas might look like.

"Listen, people all over the world do this. They worry for soldiers, police officers…anyone who's in the line of danger. I'm sure they're able to figure out how to compartmentalize their worries. It's just something you need to think about as you move forward."

"One problem at a time." Mirra blew out a breath and went to sit at the table with her food. "I need to keep him safe. And I have to get him to accept me."

"Those are two big hurdles."

"They are." Mirra bit into her muffin, enjoying the taste of the jam. "I'm confident I can do this. It's just… I wish it could be easier."

"That's not the hand you've been dealt. Are you going to fold or play the game?"

"Play."

"Good. Because it's your next move. I'll just go let Silas in," Irma said, then nodded when the doorbell rang.

"He's here?" Mirra glanced down at her loose tank top and ragged sleep shorts in dismay. "How did you know?"

Irma just tapped a finger to her head and smiled before disappearing from the kitchen. There wasn't much Mirra could do about her appearance at this point, so she just scowled and finished her English muffin. She was wiping the jam from her fingers when Splash bounded into the kitchen.

"Splash! Hey, handsome!" Mirra bent to pet the excited dog, who all but climbed her legs. "Sure, you can come up."

Silas stopped in the doorway when he saw her cradling Splash in her arms. "He was, ah, pretty insistent about coming back here."

"Is that right? But not you?" Mirra asked, raising an eyebrow at Silas over Splash's head.

"Ah, well." Silas looked around the kitchen, his eyes scanning, always scanning. "Is there someplace we can talk in private?"

"It's here or my bedroom. We have guests in the garden."

"I guess your bedroom then."

Surprised by his choice, Mirra only nodded and stood, carrying Splash with her through the cool hallway to her bedroom. She nudged the door open with her foot and entered. A naturally neat person, Mirra had automatically made her bed when she woke up, but her eyes still caught on the hot-pink lace bra that hung from its drying rack by her balcony. She wasn't embarrassed about wearing pretty underwear, though, and a quick scan of her room showed nothing out of order.

She'd designed the room in cool soothing tones, like the mist hovering over the water at dawn. The walls were painted with an ombre effect, starting from a deep blue and graduating all the way down to white. The rug was a light blue with undulating waves of white and had a shaggy texture that was soft on her feet. Mirra sat on the corner of her bed and dug her toes into the rug, her heart hammering in her chest.

"I don't have much time," Silas began as he sat next to her on the bed. The mattress dipped a little with his weight, and Mirra found herself leaning closer to him. "Prince called. The drop is happening just after sunset. I guess they want to do it while other boats might be on the water. To make it look less obvious? I'm not sure of the reasoning."

"Prince's information is fairly reliable." Mirra stroked Splash, pressing her cheek to the dog's fur so that her face was turned to Silas. He looked tired, she realized, and more than a little bit sad.

"Yes, well, so far he's been a help. I have no reason to believe he'd set me up. But I'm struggling to believe a lot of things right now." Silas met her eyes.

Mirra could see the emotions that teemed inside of him. Confusion. Sadness. Anger. And...yet.

"Silas, can you tell me why you walked away from me the other night?"

"I..." Silas pinched the bridge of his nose and took a deep breath. "It's hard to explain."

"Try me."

"As I said, I don't have much time."

Mirra feared his words carried a deeper meaning. If he was hurt tonight, would their time run out? Desperate to make a connection with him, she leaned closer and put her hand on his leg.

"Silas. Please talk to me," Mirra whispered.

"I feel like I'm going crazy." Silas stared at her hand on his leg. "All I do is think about you. And yet at the same time, it feels like my world is falling apart and I can't trust anyone."

Mirra's heart had soared when he said he thought about her. "You can trust me."

"Can I?" Silas was still staring at her hand. "I want to. I really want to, Mirra. But I don't know if you're…"

"Stable? Sane?" Mirra suggested when his words trailed off.

"I'm sorry. It sounds incredibly rude when you say it like that."

"Why did you come here then? If you thought I was insane?"

"Because I like you, Mirra. I can't stop thinking about you. At your core, I know you're a good person. I've decided that if you believe you're a mermaid…well, that's okay with me."

"Oh, well, thank you very much." Mirra huffed out a laugh, unsure of whether to take this as a small win from him or to be royally offended. "You've decided to just accept that I'm insane and go from there?"

"How about 'eccentric'?" Silas finally met her eyes. "We're all a little odd, don't you think? Those of us who end up on this island? I can't say I've got it all together either."

"I feel like you're humoring me."

"It's the only way to make sense of what you've told me. I…I don't know how else to accept it."

Patience, Jolie had told her. The sun was setting, the cartel was making its move, and Silas had nobody to turn to. She could make this a sticking point right now, or she could hear the man out.

"How about this – can you promise me to keep an open mind and we can revisit this discussion at another time?"

When Silas reached out and put his hand over hers and squeezed, Mirra closed her eyes and took a deep breath.

"I can do that," Silas said.

Mirra suspected it was a huge concession on his part.

"Silas, I…care for you," Mirra said, leaning closer to him. "I wouldn't lie to you. We don't have to talk about it now, but I can't let you leave without you knowing how I feel about you."

"You shouldn't care for me, Mirra." Silas's eyes were drenched in sadness when they met hers. "I have nothing to give anyone."

"Sure you do. You're smart. Handsome. Caring. You have a lot to give."

"I don't know how to…do this," Silas made a circle motion with his finger in the air. "Be with you. Be a part of your family. You've got this built-in core of relationships that I have no idea how to navigate. I've always been a lone wolf. I don't know how to look after anyone else."

"You look after Splash." Splash looked over his shoulder at his name.

"Not very well, obviously. He got stolen, remember?"

"That's not your fault. Nobody could have prevented that."

"I should have."

"You're pretty hard on yourself, aren't you?" Mirra's eyes searched Silas's face for any sign of self-compassion. Instead, if possible, his face grew even harder.

"I have to be. Nobody else is going to look out for me."

"I can look out for you. If you'll let me," Mirra whispered.

"Mirra…" Silas's eyes widened when Mirra bent and put Splash on the floor. Turning, she stood in front of Silas, pushing herself between his open legs. As if of their own accord, his hands settled at her waist. Mirra drew him closer, though he resisted for a moment, until finally he let her hug him. She stroked his hair as he pressed his face to her abdomen, his arms tight around her.

"You don't have to be so tough all the time," Mirra whispered. "Leaning on other people makes you strong too."

"How?" Silas's voice was muffled against her, the timbre of it sending chills up her skin.

"Because the strongest tree isn't the one that holds rigid in the storm. The one that survives knows when to bend. Bend a little, Silas. You don't have to be on guard all the time."

"It's all I know. I…I've never been able to rely on anyone else. If I let myself down…if I ask for help…what do I have then? I can't even trust my own self."

"You're not meant to be a master at everything."

"I'm a master at staying alive. At landing on my feet."

"Yes, you're surviving, Silas. Well done, you. But are you living?"

At that, Silas tilted his head up to meet her eyes. Helpless not to touch him, Mirra ran her hands down the side of his face. He was so handsome and there was still so much hurt inside him. She wanted to be the one to fill his void, to make him feel whole again.

"You make me believe…that maybe things could be

different," Silas said, and that was enough for Mirra. For now.

Bending over, she brought her lips to his, still cupping his face, and the moment drew out. Suspended in time, they stayed like that, wrapped around each other, as each person allowed a bit of their walls to crumble.

"I have to go," Silas said, pulling back. Sadness still hung in his eyes, but now it warred with a healthy amount of lust. "I need to get to the boat."

"I understand." Mirra stepped back and her eyes trailed up his body as he stood, just inches from her. Once more, she wrapped her arms around him for a hug. "Please be safe. Don't do anything stupid. Don't be the hero."

"I have a favor to ask of you."

Mirra noted that he didn't promise her anything about his own personal safety. "What's that?"

"Can I leave Splash here? I don't want to leave him at the office again. I'm worried the boat won't be safe. And I figure that since they already took him once and we got him back, they won't try it again. You should be safe. I'm hoping, at least."

"Of course. I can also bring more people over tonight. We have quite a few people who love us. Should I call my friends over?"

"That might be smart. Safety in numbers. If this does go down tonight, I'll feel better not having to worry about you on your own."

Mirra didn't mention that she wouldn't be the one at home watching Splash. But she was certain that, if she called Sam and Lucas and a few others over, Splash would be more than safe while she trailed Silas's boat.

"I'll call them as soon as you leave. I don't mind asking for help when it's needed."

Mirra only smiled at Silas's pointed look. "Isn't asking you to watch Splash asking for help?"

"It is!" Mirra exclaimed, and stepped back to pat him on the arm. "There's promise for you yet, young Jedi."

"I should find you annoying," Silas said, a smile hovering on his lips. Mirra loved when he smiled, as he did so quite infrequently.

"But you don't. Instead you're intrigued, even if you think I'm delusional."

"Maybe the crazy ones are just more fun?" Silas ducked when Mirra pretended to swat him on the head.

"You'd better get out of here before you find out how a woman actually reacts to being called crazy when, in fact, she is not. However" – Mirra held up a hand to forestall Silas – "I know you're new to this relationship stuff so I'll give you a pass. I'm willing to teach you."

"That sounds…promising." Heat flashed through Silas's look and Mirra gasped as he grabbed her and gave her a searing kiss.

"Please stay safe tonight?" Mirra asked as Silas bent to pet Splash.

"I'll do my best. I'll be back in the morning for Splash. The bag I gave Irma has food and treats."

"He'll be pampered like a king, I promise."

"No wonder he's been whining to get back here."

"I suspect he's trying to tell you something. But you're not ready to hear it." Mirra only raised an eyebrow at Silas when he shot her another one of his looks. Oh, yeah. She was getting good at navigating this man's roadblocks. His walls were coming down whether he liked it or not.

"Good night, Mirra. I'll see you in the morning."

"Be safe, Silas." Mirra crouched and held Splash when he would have followed Silas out the door. The dog looked up at her in question.

"Don't worry, Splash. I'm going to take care of him, no matter what."

CHAPTER 20

"You are not going alone." Irma leveled a look at Mirra.

"Of course she's not," Jolie said as she sauntered into the kitchen.

"You both need to stay here and watch Splash," Mirra argued.

"We most certainly do not. Splash is going next door with Lucas and Samantha. Pipin and Snowy will play with him, and Lucas is more than well-equipped enough to handle any threats. Plus!" Irma held up a finger when Mirra opened her mouth to speak. "They would think to come here for Splash. Not next door."

"But what about our guests?" Mirra asked. "Aren't you putting them in danger by not being here in case something does happen?"

Torn, Jolie and Irma looked at each other.

"I think I have to do this alone," Mirra said, looking from one of them to the other. "It's not that I don't want your help. Trust me, we could probably use all the help we can get. But I think I have to be the one to go."

"I don't like this," Irma said, crossing the kitchen and pulling Mirra into her arms. "I really don't like this."

"I'll be safe. It's not me you should worry about."

"You'll bring him to us?" Irma asked.

"If he gets hurt, I don't know what I'll do."

"If he's really hurt, Mirra, you know where to take him."

"Oh, yes, because that worked out so well for you and Ted."

"I mean, he panicked a bit, sure. But he came around. Now he's always wheedling invitations back home out of me." Jolie tossed her hair and laughed. "He calls it Mermaid Nirvana."

"I mean, for someone like him it probably *is* nirvana." Mirra smiled as they spoke about their home far beneath the waves, where the other mermaids lived. Their family had been granted special access to land, as Mirra and Jolie's father had been human. The magick was strong in their underwater village, and Mirra knew that help received there could defy the laws of physics. It would be a last resort, but one she'd use if it would save Silas's life.

"Take him there if you need to. They will help."

"Let's hope we can stop this before it gets that far. So, it's agreed? You'll both stay?" Mirra stopped at the doorway and waited for their answers.

"We'll stay. Call for us if you need us."

Mirra accepted hugs from both women, but her mind was already with Silas. The sun was hovering close to the horizon and she knew she didn't have much time to get there.

There were guests on the beach, so Mirra left through the front door and walked a ways down the road until she found a little path that wound around a row of palm trees and to the beach. When she was certain she was no longer in anyone's sight, Mirra shed her clothes and streaked across the sand to dive into the water.

Once she'd changed into her mermaid form, Mirra didn't dally to check on her turtles or swim past her reefs. She made a beeline for the harbor, where she knew Silas would be getting on his boat. By the time she had reached the harbor, the sun had disappeared and darkness cloaked her movements. Mirra peeked her head up from the water to scan.

The Marine Enforcement boats had just left the harbor and were heading out in different directions across the water. Mirra sighted Silas's boat and took off after it. It looked like they were heading south. And by "they," Mirra meant Silas and a second Marine Enforcement boat that seemed to be keeping pace with him. She wondered if they were going to the same beach or if one would stop along the way. The southern part of Siren Island was the most remote, which meant it made sense for it to be the location of a drop from the drug cartel. It would take police ages to get there by land.

Nerves worked their way through Mirra as she kept pace with the boats, opting to dive deep beneath the surface and swimming along below them in the darkness. While it could be a risk to travel largely underwater – something might happen suddenly on the surface – Mirra was more worried that one of the boats would spot her if she swam too often at the surface.

When they neared the southernmost point, the engines slowed. Perhaps the captain had sent two boats to monitor this location because it took the longest to get to. It made sense, and yet something about having the second Marine Enforcement boat there put Mirra on edge. She still wasn't sure the captain was trustworthy, and if he had secondary motives – well, this would be a good spot to take care of them.

Once the motors cut, Mirra swam in a large circle beneath the boats, then surfaced silently behind one. No sound greeted her. There was no communication between the boats and they had cut the running lights. Aside from the occasional lap of water against the hull of the boat, the night was silent. It was a new moon, so very little light shone across the dark sea. Mirra moved silently to position herself at the back of Silas's boat, out of the line of sight of the other one. It wouldn't be good to be spotted right now.

It wasn't long before the whine of a plane engine cut through the night. Mirra felt the boat shift as Silas padded silently to the bow.

It happened fast, much faster than Mirra had antici- pated. As the plane drew near, Mirra squinted into the sky, but the plane was flying without its lights on so she could go on sound only. Several large splashes sounded, and she realized the plane had dropped the large drums it carried into the water.

Seeing her chance for distraction, Mirra dove beneath the boat and surfaced near a drum that was bobbing on the surface of the sea. Already she could hear that the Jet Skis had started up.

There was silence from both boats, and she realized they were waiting until the Jet Skis drew closer before taking any action. Grabbing the rope of one of the drums, Mirra dove beneath the surface to hide herself and swam in the opposite direction of the boats as fast as she could. Adrenaline raced through her. She wanted to be in two places at once, but wasn't sure if what she was doing was smart or wildly screwing up the plan. Mirra let go of the drum's rope and swam several yards away, surfacing but keeping low to the water.

Shouts broke out across the water as the Jet Skis zipped around in confusion. Mirra's heart jumped to her throat when she heard a shot ring out across the water. It was difficult to see, as none of the watercraft had their lights on, and the scant starlight did little to help illuminate the scene. Mirra gasped as one of the Jet Skis zipped by close to her head, and she ducked beneath the water.

Swimming beneath the surface, Mirra stayed low so she wouldn't get caught by any of the propellers. When she surfaced again, as luck would have it, she was by another drum. This time she grabbed the drum and dragged it in the other direction. She started moving in a circular motion, hoping to create chaos and confuse the drug lords. Faster and faster she moved, swirling in a circle, until all the Jet Skis had come to a stop by the drum. Then Mirra dove far more deeply than before and swam to the other side of the boats, hoping to be clear of the confusion she'd deliberately created.

When a spotlight hit her directly in the face, Mirra

froze, momentarily blinded, and threw an arm up to shield her eyes. Instinctively, she dropped below the surface and once again kept to the darkness. It would do no good for her to be seen at this point. The cartel members were already confused, and Silas didn't need to be distracted by her. When a bullet whizzed past her, cutting neatly through the water, Mirra darted to the side and zipped away, hoping Silas could momentarily fend for himself until she could circle back and out of the light.

She hoped he hadn't seen her.

Heart racing, Mirra began to call with her magick.

CHAPTER 21

or a heart-stopping second, Silas thought he saw Mirra silhouetted in the beam of the strobe light he'd flipped on. His eyes widened, and he blinked to adjust to the suddenness of the light shining through the darkness.

This was why women were trouble, Silas decided, shaking his head and ducking low on the boat as he assessed the situation. Even at the worst possible times they popped into your head. What he *should* be doing was trying to not get shot at. And he'd stood there, a virtual target on his chest, blinking madly at the surface of the water, convinced he'd seen a mermaid.

Now, shouts broke across the water and Silas heard more than one shot being fired. Keeping his head low, he hovered at the bow, a gun in hand. Pressing the radio to his mouth, he opened communication.

"Shots fired. Southernmost point. Request backup immediately."

Silas watched as men on Jet Skis shouted at each other,

confusion and chaos seeming to take charge. Even for him, seeing the drums full of drugs moving in different directions had been disorienting. Now the men turned on each other, standing tall on their Jet Skis, shouting orders and pointing fingers. Silas brought his gun up.

The cold steel of a gun barrel pressed against his neck. Closing his eyes, Silas sucked in his breath.

"Drop it."

"Who are you?"

"Drop the gun and kick it away."

Silas let out a shaky breath as his stomach turned over. He knew this voice. When he turned, he'd be staring a traitor in the face.

Dropping his gun, he kicked it away so that it slid across the deck of his boat. Knowing well enough not to move unless ordered to, Silas waited, his neck cranked away from the press of the gun.

"I want you to turn around and stand up. Slowly!" the voice barked.

Silas gripped the railing and slowly pulled himself up, his heart plummeting as he saw the Jet Skis making off with the shipment of drugs. All of this would be for nothing, he realized, aside from losing his life. He hadn't even had a chance to stop the trafficking. Regret crept through him. Was this the end of it all? Everything he had worked for? All the times he'd pulled himself up from the gutter? For what – to be betrayed by someone he'd called a friend and to go to his death never knowing true happiness?

He couldn't say that, Silas realized. He'd had some moments. Splash made him happy. There was nothing finer than a calm day on the water with Splash at his side.

Mirra's face flashed in his mind once more. Maybe he should've taken more of a chance there. At least he'd die having known the taste of her on his lips. Now he'd never know what they might have been.

He'd never find out if mermaids were real.

That thought alone filled him with rage, so that when he turned and lifted his gaze to look at his traitor, Silas knew his eyes burned with hate.

"Ronaldo."

"Ah, Silas. *Mi amigo*." Ronaldo grinned.

"No, we are not friends." Silas bit out.

"You wound me." Ronaldo grinned even wider, the light of greed glinting in his eyes. It wasn't insanity in Ronaldo's eyes, but just pure avarice.

This wasn't the same light he'd seen in Mirra's eyes when she'd looked at him. The difference was startling, and Silas suddenly understood that Mirra had looked at him with love. The concept was so foreign to Silas that he had assumed she must be crazy. Crazy to take a chance on someone like him. Crazy to think that she saw some good in him when he felt like he'd been dead inside for years. But around her, he hadn't been. Oh no – all of him had lit up inside. It had scared him, the heat of his emotions, and he'd thought he might die if he let them burn. But now, facing actual death, he realized how foolish he'd been all along.

Because life came from freedom.

Freedom from letting his past control his future. Freedom to choose his own direction. Freedom to take a chance that his path could be different. Silas didn't want the shell of the life he'd been living anymore. He wanted a life full of mermaids, laughter, and love. He wanted to take risks and make friends and…well, to live.

Now he just had to figure out how to make it happen.

"What are you doing, Ronaldo? If you say we're friends, why are you doing this?"

"Ah, it's simple, *mi amigo*. You see…" Ronaldo smiled his crazy smile at him once more.

"Money."

"You win! Yes, the money. I needed the money. My wife's family is hurting. I am in debt. Life would be much easier with the money. It was too good to pass up, what they were offering."

"How much is my life worth to you?"

"Five hundred thousand dollars."

"I'm surprised you didn't push them for a million." Silas decided to needle him a bit while he shifted closer to the railing.

"Five hundred thousand is a lot of money. More than you have. It will make me rich." Ronaldo glared at him.

"These guys have millions. You could've pushed for more."

"You have no idea what you're talking about," Ronaldo bit out, the smile dropping from his face.

"Maybe you keep a drum of your own? Sell some of it? That way you can make even more money."

Ronaldo stared at him for a moment, and then laughed. "Oh, you had me going for a moment there, man. Yes, yes, you did. I see you are trying to push my buttons."

"I'm not. Just wondering what's motivating you."

"I told you. The money was too good to refuse. This should have been simple and quiet, except you had to go and capture those fishermen. They talked. But they have now been silenced, of course."

Silas's eyes widened as he realized Ronaldo had just confessed to murder. "I didn't capture the fishermen. I saved the blond, remember?"

"Ah yes – she's a tasty snack, isn't she?"

At that, Silas jerked forward involuntarily.

Ronaldo laughed. "Oh man, you've got it bad. Maybe I'll find her tonight and have my way with her."

"You'll have bigger problems on your hands."

"Like what? I'm out of here tonight, amigo. I'm helping them move it."

"You don't think they'll track you?"

"We've got better intel. Money talks. Something you wouldn't understand. You always have to follow the rules."

"Rules are meant to be followed." Silas shrugged and inched farther backward.

"Listen to yourself! What a little schoolboy you are. You always bothered me, you know. With your perfect attendance, your little house with no furniture. What are you living for, man? For work? You don't even spend your money. What's the point? I was going to try to cut you in, but I knew I'd never turn you. You're too straitlaced. Mr. Perfect."

"I'm far from perfect, man. You have to know that."

"You try to be. You suck up to the Captain all the time."

"I respect the captain. It's part of our duty."

"Listen to you!"

"It was you with the captain, wasn't it? I just realized it. You went back for your radio that night."

Ronaldo laughed. "Yes, it was me. Sorry about that."

"You stole my dog, you sick piece of shit." Silas narrowed his eyes at Ronaldo.

"Hey, man, I didn't hurt him. Even my cold dead heart wouldn't hurt a dog. I hope you left him somewhere nice, because he's going to go real hungry when you don't come home tonight."

"This isn't necessary, Ronaldo." Silas wasn't going to plead for his life – it just wasn't in his nature. But maybe he could reason. "If the drug lords turn on you, you'll just be adding murder to your charges."

Ronaldo waved the gun in the air. "If the drug lords turn on you…" he said in a high-pitched voice, mimicking Silas. "They won't turn on me, you idiot. They need me."

"You haven't learned that yet, have you?" Silas laughed, and this time Ronaldo went silent. "Don't you know the one truth about all of this?"

"What's that?" Ronaldo snapped, his face thunderous.

"Everyone's expendable." At that, Silas jumped back and threw himself over the railing. He managed to kick out as Ronaldo fired the gun, but not hard enough to completely foul Ronaldo's shot. The bullet hit him hard in the side, like a burning knife to the gut.

The last thing he saw as he hit the dark water was Mirra's horrified face.

CHAPTER 22

$\mathcal{M}$irra couldn't risk taking Silas to where the mermaids lived, deep in the sea, though she could have desperately used their magick. He was bleeding out as she cradled him, just beneath the surface of the water, and she knew her time was limited. She pulled Silas to her and pressed her lips to his, forcing his mouth open and breathing air into his lungs. She was already moving, pulling him toward the second most magickal place she knew, and the closest to where they were.

The Cave of Souls.

Mirra's terror was palpable and her dolphin friends read her energy, coming from the depths to surround her and propel her and Silas forward. Precious seconds ticked by as Mirra swam harder than she ever had before, refusing to pause as she repeatedly blew air into Silas's mouth, panic lancing her gut. If she didn't make it in time, if he lost too much blood, even her magick wouldn't be able to save him.

Surfacing at the small island with the Cave of Souls,

Mirra dragged Silas to the beach and allowed herself to transform. Wrapping her magick around her like a cloak, Mirra used it to help her pull Silas's prone form into the protection of the cave. Once there, Mirra dropped to her knees next to him to assess his condition. Water trickled down her body, dripping on Silas as she bent over him.

Around them, hundreds of pearls in all shapes and sizes were clustered together. A shaft of moonlight shone through a crack in the cave, illuminating the pearls and creating a soft, lustrous glow in the cavern. The magick here was strong, a universal life force that hummed around Mirra.

"Silas," she whispered, "I'm here for you. I won't leave you."

"Mirra?" He opened his eyes and blinked at her, and Mirra's heart stuttered in her chest. "What…"

"Shhh, don't talk. Please just save your energy. You've been seriously injured."

"Where…"

"Shhh."

"Mirra." Silas tried to reach for her and Mirra took his hand, pressing it to her heart. "Don't leave me. Everyone leaves…"

Silas's lids fluttered shut and his head dropped to the side, and Mirra knew he'd lost consciousness. She dropped his hand and pressed her palms to the wound in his side, where blood gushed out at a rate too fast for survival.

"Do you love him?"

Mirra glanced up to see the oracle, in her human form, standing by Silas. She held a glowing pearl in her hand.

"Is that his soul?" Mirra whispered, dread taking her breath away.

"It is."

"Please, can you help him?"

"You didn't answer my question."

"I do love him, yes."

"He's not professed his love for you yet." The oracle turned the pearl in her hands, the glow emanating from Silas's soul illuminating the angles of the oracle's face.

"He hasn't, no," Mirra said.

"Do you understand what this means? If I help you?"

"I don't...not really." Mirra's eyes dropped back to Silas's limp body. Time was going by too fast, and she was worried he wouldn't come back. "But please, can you help him?"

"If I give this soul to you," the oracle continued, unhurried, "it will be yours to protect."

"I understand that."

"You only get one soul to watch over, Mirra. You aren't the protector of lost souls. You don't have that type of magick."

Mirra blinked at her. "What are you saying?"

"That if I give you his soul, then that's it. He's yours to protect and watch over for life."

"Yes, I understand that."

"Even," the oracle said, her tone gentle, her eyes glowing white, "if he doesn't love you back."

Mirra paused, finally understanding what the oracle was trying to tell her. If she saved Silas's life, she would carry his soul for protection, and there would be no room for another love in her life. If he didn't ever love her back, she'd live a life alone, devoid of love. Romantic love, at least.

It was a huge decision to make, and would be based on very little knowledge of how Silas would react to her when he came to. Her thoughts tangled in her mind. Mirra blinked down at him, tears filling her eyes. She didn't know if he loved her – if he even *could* love her – let alone whether he'd ever be able to accept her for who and what she was.

It was a huge risk.

But wasn't that what love was? Mirra asked herself. Love was jumping into the abyss and hoping someone would catch her. All she could trust right now were her own feelings, and she knew she loved Silas. Deep in the very marrow of her bones, Mirra could feel the love for him coursing through her. Even if he couldn't love her back, maybe she could love enough for the both of them.

Everyone leaves…

Silas's words drifted back to her. He'd lived a life of abandonment. Now he expected and accepted that everyone would leave him. Not once had somebody stood for him. But she could.

Mirra looked up and met the oracle's gaze. "I understand what you are telling me. I'm willing to take the risk. I love him and I'm asking you to give his soul to me to protect. Forever. My love will not waver. Even if he can't love me back."

"Then it is so."

The oracle reached out and lifted the pearl necklace at Mirra's throat. There was a flash of power, and Mirra gasped as she felt the cool gem become infused with warmth. At the same time, a soft hum of energy surrounded them. Reaching out, Mirra plucked a thread of the life energy from the air, a golden tendril, and brought it to Silas's wound. The oracle kneeled next to her, entwining her hands with Mirra's, and together they fused their power to flood Silas's body with healing energy.

When it was done, the oracle stepped back. "It won't be enough to completely heal him. He'll still need time to recover. I assume you'll see to him in the next days while he heals?"

"Of course. I'll bring him home. Is it safe for me to swim with him?"

"The bleeding has stopped and we've removed the bullet. The wound has knit, but be careful on your swim home; it can reopen. He's a lucky man."

"Thank you, oracle. Your magick humbles me."

"You've received your gift, child. I can only hope you've made the right choice."

With that, the oracle disappeared and Mirra was left alone with Silas, the soft light of the Cave of Souls enveloping them in a cocoon of warmth and positive energy. His chest rose and fell steadily, and Mirra took just a moment to get her bearings. Gratitude filled her that he was alive, but she understood the gravity of the choice she'd made. Could this man bring himself to love her? Mirra studied the sharp angles of his face and hoped that the depth of her love would be enough for them both.

Now to get him home.

Tapping into the power of the cave, Mirra pushed her arms beneath Silas and brought him to her chest, cradling him as she backed awkwardly from the cave and dragged him toward the beach. Her magick made her strong, but the cave made her stronger. If she'd been on her own, it was likely she'd have torn his wound right back open as she clumsily dragged his body back to the water.

But what she lacked in finesse she made up for in speed, and soon she was waist-deep in the water. Calling upon her magick, Mirra changed once more into her mermaid form and nestled Silas's back against her chest.

"Mirra?" Silas turned to look over his shoulder at her, his eyes cloudy with pain and confusion.

"Shh. Just rest, Silas. I've got you."

"You stayed…"

"I'll always stay. Rest now, Silas."

Mirra didn't want to risk him becoming more alert and struggling against her. She took off into the night, Silas secure at her chest, her dolphin army surrounding her as they began the trek home.

Sirens broke the stillness of the night, and Mirra watched as boats raced across the water, presumably toward where they'd left Ronaldo and the drugs. Had it been only moments that they'd been inside the Cave of Souls? It felt like hours. Floodlights flashed across the water, but Mirra was far enough away that the light didn't touch her. She could only hope Ronaldo would be captured and held accountable for what he'd done.

When they drew close to the Laughing Mermaid, the dolphins backed off, disappearing once more into the depths as Mirra waded to shore. Jolie and Irma raced into the water, reaching for Silas as Mirra completed her transformation back to human. Together, the three of them carried Silas to the beach.

"How far gone is he?" Irma demanded.

"The oracle healed him. We just need to get him to a bed. He'll need a few days to recuperate if we can keep him still."

Mirra's head shot up as a bullet of fur raced across the beach and skidded to a stop at Silas's side. Splash began licking his face, little whimpers emanating from his trembling body.

"Splash, he's okay. He'll be okay. I promise." Mirra bent to pet the dog's head.

"Splash." Silas shook his head back and forth to escape the dog's tongue on his face. "Buddy."

"Do you think he can walk if he's lucid?" Irma asked, her hands on her hips as she studied him.

Silas shook his head again and then blinked up at three of them. "Am I in heaven?" he asked.

"No. Why?"

"Boobs," Silas said, and pointed to them. It was at that moment that Mirra realized all three of them were naked, having just changed from their mermaid forms, as Irma and Jolie had disregarded Mirra's demand that they not join the rescue mission. Leave it to a man to focus on *that* detail and not the fact that he was alive.

"Right, then. If you're good enough to ogle breasts, you're good enough to walk. Up and at 'em," Irma ordered, hoisting Silas up by his arm. Together, they hauled Silas inside, Jolie's shoulders shaking with laughter the entire way.

"Jolie, I swear to goddess…" Mirra hissed.

"Relax," Jolie laughed. "It's a good sign. He's going to be just fine."

CHAPTER 23

Silas slept clear through the next day, and so did Mirra, curled up on a lounge chair next to his bed. They'd put him in a guestroom, and while the bed would have been more comfortable for Mirra, it didn't feel right to join him there without his permission. Instead, they'd placed a chair next to the bed for her. She'd wrapped a shell-pink sarong around her body before tumbling headfirst into a sleep so deep she didn't dream at all.

"Mirra?"

She blinked her eyes open, sitting up and immediately leaning toward the bed.

"Silas. Here, don't move." Mirra reached for the jug of water by the bed and poured him a glass. "Just sip. You've been through a lot."

"I…" Silas's voice was raspy and he shook his head as if to clear the fuzziness from his brain. Grasping the glass, he took his time sipping the water, his cool grey eyes on hers over the rim. Once he'd sated himself, he handed the glass back to her and Mirra placed it on the table by his bed.

"How do you feel?" she asked, standing up and reaching to pull the bed sheet down to check his wound.

Silas grabbed it before she could. "It appears I am naked," he said by way of explanation.

"Yes, you are," Mirra said. "Your clothes were covered in blood."

"Ah." Lifting the sheet so only he could see, he looked down at his chest. "It also appears I have a very large wound, based on the size of the bandage."

"Yes, you do. You'll need to spend several days recovering."

"Why am I not in a hospital, Mirra?"

"You didn't need one." She didn't elaborate. She couldn't be certain of everything he remembered.

Silas blinked at her before raising an eyebrow. "If I remember correctly – and I feel like I do, because the pain was unbearable – I was shot at nearly point-blank range."

"Correct."

"And you're saying I didn't need the hospital?"

"Also correct."

Confusion crossed Silas's face and he opened his mouth to speak again, but a soft knock sounded at the door.

"Come in," Mirra said, grateful for the interruption. Her heart was hammering in her chest and she had no idea how to explain to Silas how he'd healed so quickly. The truth, Mirra reminded herself. She had nothing to be embarrassed about. She could only offer Silas her explanation; it would be his decision whether he believed her.

"Ah, you're awake. Good. I've brought some fuel for your body." Irma entered the room wearing loose linen pants and a soft purple shirt. Her hair was bundled on top of her head, and Mirra suspected she'd spent much of the day resting as well. Irma placed a tray over Silas and held up a finger when he started to speak. "You'll look ungrateful that we saved your life if you don't let us take care of you. Is that what you want?"

"No, ma'am." Silas pressed his lips together.

"Good. I've got some vegetable soup here, a home-made biscuit, and some tea. None of this is spicy, but it should be enough to give you some sustenance to start. I expect you to eat it all and not give Mirra any fuss about it."

"Yes, ma'am," Silas said again.

"I've been in contact with Captain Reid. He sends his best and knows you are in good hands. I'll collect the tray later. Go on, eat up." With that, Irma sailed from the room. As Mirra was about to speak, she returned with another tray.

"You don't have to serve me," Mirra protested. "I could've come to the kitchen and gotten food."

"You had a tough night too. Relax." Irma placed the tray next to her on the lounge chair, then bent and pressed a kiss to Mirra's cheek.

"Formidable woman," Silas said, once he was certain Irma was out of earshot.

"The best women usually are." Mirra smiled.

"I'm surprised to admit it, but I'm famished."

"Dig in. I'm hungry as well."

They ate in silence for a moment, both too hungry and

too tired to do much more than focus on the single task of feeding themselves. Once Mirra felt sated, she pushed the tray aside and stood. "I'll be right back."

"Wait...where are you going?"

"I need to use the bathroom, if you must know." Mirra smiled and picked up her tray.

"Oh, right, sorry."

"I won't be long. Finish your food."

Mirra disappeared with the tray and stopped just outside the kitchen door. Leaning against the wall, she took a deep breath, and then another. She needed a moment to center herself. She had no idea how the next few minutes with Silas would go and it felt like her future hung by a thread. Her nerves tingled, and it had taken all of her effort to force some food into her body.

After pushing the door open to the kitchen, Mirra stopped when Irma turned from where she stood stirring a pot on the stove, Splash at her feet.

"Oh honey, it'll be just fine," Irma said, moving across the room to wrap her arms around Mirra. "No matter what happens. You've got us."

"And if he doesn't love me?" Mirra asked, leaning into her mother's warmth.

"Then you live a happy life anyway. It might not be the life you've dreamed of, but it can still be a happy one. Just look at me."

Her mother was right. Irma had lived a solitary life, raising her two daughters, and creating a fulfilling and satisfying world for herself. She loved others freely, nurtured everyone she came across, and had built a tight circle of friends. Though Irma didn't have a partner, she certainly didn't lack for love.

"You're right. You're absolutely right. Romantic love isn't the only way one can live a deeply meaningful life. I'm sorry if I've offended you," Mirra said, pulling back to study her mother's eyes.

"You haven't. I wish for you the love that I wasn't able to have, but I also know you have the softest heart of all of us. You're just caught up in this right now and you can't see that you'll be okay no matter what happens. I understand that. I deeply understand that. But try to understand that even if Silas walks away from you, you'll live a rich and bountiful life. And I will be right by your side, making sure that you do."

"I love you," Mirra sighed.

"I love you, too, my sweetest child. Go to him now. And take Splash. The dog loves me, but he misses Silas."

"Of course. That will make him feel better." Mirra straightened her shoulders and, with Splash at her heels, she returned to Silas's bedroom. Bending over, she picked Splash up before she entered the room and could feel excitement course through the dog when he spotted Silas on the bed.

"Splash!" Silas said, his face lighting up. For a brief moment, Mirra found herself jealous of a dog. She wished Silas would look at *her* that way. After gently putting Splash on the bed, Mirra removed the now-empty tray so Silas could gather the dog into his arms. Splash licked Silas's face and Silas pulled him tight. "I'm glad you're safe, buddy."

"Not only is he safe, but he's going to get fat if he

keeps hanging out in our kitchen. My mother is shameless about feeding him."

"Uh-oh. We'll have to put you in doggy boot camp," Silas laughed, stroking the dog's fur. Looking up, he smiled at Mirra in such an open way that it took her breath away for a moment. "Thank you for keeping him safe. I don't know what I'd do if he'd gotten hurt."

"You are most welcome. He's had a grand time cavorting with Pipin and getting snacks from Irma."

"You'll spoil him in no time."

Mirra's nerves screamed in her stomach. When was he going to bring up what had happened? There was no way he could have missed seeing her mermaid form. Perhaps the pain had been too much and he'd blocked out the memories? But he'd just said he remembered being shot.

"He deserves a little spoiling. He's a good dog, Silas."

"The best. Mirra…I have a question for you. And I hate to ask this."

"Yes?" Mirra's eyes widened as she waited.

"I don't know that I'm going to be steady on my feet, but I would very much like to visit the restroom…if you could help me get up?"

"Oh, of course." Mirra stood up, then paused when Silas grimaced at her as he leaned forward. "Too much pain?"

"It hurts, I'll admit. But I also forgot I'm naked."

"Right." Mirra turned and handed him a sarong that sat on a chest of drawers.

"A skirt?"

"Many men wear sarongs. Particularly traditional islanders."

"I'll take it. I guess I'm manly enough to pull it off."

Silas took the sarong from her and, sitting up, tied it around his waist before pushing the sheet off and swinging his legs over the side. He paused, his head bent, and she realized he must be lightheaded. Mirra reached out and slid her hand under his muscular bicep, and waited while he gathered himself.

When he finally stood, Mirra just about swallowed her tongue. A man in a sarong should not look as sexy as he did, she decided, but it was almost impossible to ignore the way the muscles rippled across his chest and down over his abdomen, ending in a V where the cotton was knotted. Dragging her eyes up, she kept them focused forward as they walked slowly to the bathroom door.

"I can take it from here."

"You're sure?"

"Yes, I'm sure," Silas said curtly, and closed the door in her face.

Well, then, Mirra thought as she made a face at Splash, who tilted his head at her and waited patiently on the bed. When Silas opened the door again, she raised her eyebrows at the look on his face.

"What's wrong?"

"Everything hurts," Silas admitted.

"I can imagine. It's not every day you take a bullet. Let's get you horizontal again and we'll see about getting you some pain meds."

"No medication," Silas said as they inched back toward the bed. "I don't like it."

"But it'll ease the pain," Mirra protested.

"No. I won't take it. It clouds the brain."

"Fine, don't take it," Mirra said with a sigh. She lowered Silas to the bed, shaking her head at the pain on his face. "Be in pain."

"There's nothing wrong with pain," Silas said as he settled back on the pillow. "It just shows you the parts you need to heal."

Mirra was about to respond, but he had already dropped off to sleep, the strain of walking to the bathroom clearly having been too much. The oracle hadn't lied when she'd said he'd need time to heal, Mirra realized, and she gently pulled the sheets back over his body. Splash padded across the bed and snuggled into his side.

"Stay with Silas, buddy. I'm going to go freshen up, and I'll be back to check on him."

It appeared their conversation would have to wait for another day.

wo days later and one would think she was a prison warden, Mirra mused as Silas shot her an angry look over his cup of tea.

"I'm more than ready to go home."

Mirra smiled sweetly at Silas. "You just slept for thirty-six hours and you still need help to go to the bathroom."

"I don't actually need help. I just like it when a beautiful woman puts her arm around me," Silas grumbled. He crossed his arms over his chest and glared at her.

It was the first time he and Mirra had been able to have a proper conversation since he'd first come to, immediately after they'd brought him to the Laughing Mermaid. After some solid rest, the color had finally started to return to his face. The sleep had done him good, but Mirra could tell she would have a challenge on her hands to keep him in bed for much longer.

"How about I put my arm around you to help you to the shower? I bet that would feel nice." Mirra kept her tone soothing, as if she were placating a toddler having a temper tantrum.

"I can see myself to the bathroom on my own."

"That's fine, but if you don't mind, I'd like to remove your bandages and check your healing."

Silas almost bit out a retort, but then pressed his lips together. He nodded his assent and waited as she approached the bed and pulled the bandages from his chest.

"It's looking much better. Though I don't think there's much we can do about the scar." Mirra traced a finger over the raised red scar, which was formed vaguely in the shape of a mermaid. She wondered if that had been the oracle's intention when she'd healed Silas.

"I'm being difficult, aren't I?" Silas asked. "I should be thanking you for your help, not being rude to you about being kept in bed. I promise I'll be nicer after a shower."

"You *are* being difficult." Mirra looked up and shot him a cheeky grin. "But I've come to expect that from you. Also, name me one man who doesn't bitch and moan when he's laid up in a sickbed."

"I wasn't bitching –" Silas shook his head, a grin lighting his face for a moment. "Okay. I was bitching. I'll be better, I promise."

"Let's get you to the shower. You'll feel much better. I'm comfortable with you moving about now that the wound has healed more."

"We still have a lot to talk about." Silas met her eyes as he swung his legs over the side of the bed. Then she handed him a fresh pair of cotton shorts. "Wait – where did you get these?"

"I thought you'd be more comfortable in these but I didn't want to go to your house and rummage through your drawers, so I ran out and bought you a few pairs. You didn't seem all that fond of the sarong." Mirra had been, though. She'd had a particularly enjoyable dream about Silas in that sarong.

"I'll pay you back," Silas promised as he stood. "I'm already in your debt."

"It's not...you don't have to..." Mirra protested. She didn't touch Silas, but walked next to him as they neared the bathroom door.

"I'll pay you," Silas said, his tone brooking no argument. Mirra rolled her eyes as he shut the bathroom door in her face. Would this man never accept any kindness directed his way? It was like he viewed the world as a ledger that he always needed to keep balanced.

Mirra sat on the bed and wrapped her arm around Splash, waiting until the door opened again. Her heart did a funny little shiver as Silas opened the door and stood there in nothing but his shorts, toweling off his wet hair.

"That felt amazing. I'm feeling so much better, I'm sure I can go home now."

"Doctor's orders are that you stay for one more day of rest."

"I can do that at home."

"Fine. I'll just call Irma and let her know you're leaving." Mirra leaned forward to stand and smiled to herself when Silas grabbed her arm.

"Wait. It's just...fine. I can stay another day. But I do need to check in with the captain, and I need to give my report."

"Scared of Irma, are you?"

"Terrified." Silas winced as a brisk knock sounded on the door. An instant later, it opened.

"Did I say you could be on your feet?" Irma crossed her arms over her chest, her glare making even Mirra hunch her shoulders in defense.

"No, you didn't. I was just enjoying a shower and now I'm heading right back to bed."

"He tried to leave," Mirra said cheerfully, throwing him neatly under the bus. Silas shot her a look that would have made her cringe if she didn't know it was in his best interest to rest for another day.

"Is that right? After he shows up bloody on our doorstep and we bring him back to life? Is that how he plans to repay us, by leaving and dropping dead from exhaustion?"

"I wasn't... I don't..." Silas bowed his head and shuffled back to bed.

"One would think there'd be a little gratitude after all we've done to keep you alive." Irma sniffed, and Mirra worried she might be laying it on a little too thick.

"I *am* grateful. Immensely so. I just don't want to be a burden to you any longer." Silas caught Irma's look and all but dove under the covers of the bed.

"You'll only be a burden if you refuse our care. Or if you go home and we find you dead in your garden from sheer stubbornness. How would Splash feel if you keeled over on him?"

"I..." Silas looked from the dog to Irma.

"That's what I thought. Now, I've got a hearty chicken salad for lunch that I'll be bringing in shortly.

Will that suit, or would you like to order something fancier?"

"No, it's perfect. Thank you for taking care of me."

Mirra pressed her lips together and looked away as Irma left the room to collect lunch.

"Oh, go on and laugh. I can see your shoulders shaking."

"She put you in your place very quickly," Mirra laughed.

"Scary woman. I didn't know whether to kiss her with gratitude or run screaming for the hills. The only reason I didn't do either is I panicked. No sudden movements seemed like the best choice."

"Rightly so. You're going to have to learn to accept people mothering you."

A cloudy look passed over Silas's face, and he just shrugged one shoulder. Irma bustled back in with a tray of food for them both and shot Mirra a meaningful look.

Mirra ended up sitting next to Silas on the bed, leaning back against the abundance of plush pillows they'd laid against the headboard, listening to the sounds of the waves outside. They ate in companionable silence for a while before Silas spoke again.

"I don't know how to accept mothering."

"Silas…" Mirra turned to look at him, while he studiously stabbed another piece of his salad. "Won't you tell me about it?" She wasn't expecting him to, as he'd put up a wall with everything else she'd tried to learn about him.

"I've led a tough life, Mirra," Silas said, leaning back against the pillows. He didn't meet her eyes as he continued. "I left home very young. I should've been in school. Going to prom. Learning to drive. Having my first kiss. Instead I was basically fighting for my life. Everything was a battle. Everything. Finding food. Making money. And, still, I was one of the lucky ones."

"How so?" Mirra's heart broke for the scared little boy in Silas who had needed his mama to protect him, to bring him soup when he was sick. No wonder Irma's mothering was such a foreign concept to him.

"Because I landed a job and one of my co-workers took pity on me. He let me crash on his couch. I had a roof over my head and a safe place to sleep. He didn't make me do any funny stuff, either."

"Funny stuff?" Mirra raised an eyebrow at him.

Silas met her eyes and grimaced. "Not everyone takes advantage of younger kids. But some do." His eyes held hers until the meaning came clear.

Mirra gasped, putting a hand to her mouth. "Oh my goddess, Silas. I didn't even think about that."

"Like I said, I lucked out. I was a hard worker and Michael looked out for me. Didn't ask too many questions, but he got the gist of my story. I paid him back, too. I paid him for all the food, and the rent for using his couch. He tried to refuse it, but when I finally took off to the islands, I left it in a fat envelope on his bed so he couldn't return it to me. He's still mad at me for that." Silas laughed.

"It sounds like he wanted you to have that money as a safety net."

Silas shrugged. "I was healthy, able to work. Didn't need the safety net."

"And your mother and father?" Mirra dared to ask.

"Mom died of an overdose. I can only hope my father is dead as well."

"Oh, Silas," Mirra said. She reached for his arm, but he shrugged a shoulder to evade her touch.

"This is why I don't tell people my story. Nobody can relate. And I don't want people's pity."

"Well, no, I certainly can't relate. That's true." Mirra pushed her plate away. "I was raised without a father, but I still had a loving home. What I *can* do is empathize with your pain. But I don't pity you at all. I see a warrior. I see someone who could have taken so many dark paths, but has instead worked hard for himself and risen up to create an honorable life. I have no pity for you, Silas. Only admiration."

"Mirra…" Silas's voice was but a whisper as he turned to her with ravaged eyes. "Don't you see? I'm broken. I can tell you're interested in me. I'm not that dumb. I know when a woman has ideas. But…you're too pure. You're too good for me, Mirra. I'm only going to muddy your soul."

"And that's it? You get to decide what's best for me? What about me? Don't I have a say?" Mirra stood up and gathered up the plates, dumping them on the sideboard with a clatter. She looked around the room, but Splash had left with Irma. Mirra strode to the door and locked it, before turning to glare at Silas with her hands on her hips.

"You don't understand." A thundercloud hovered over Silas's handsome face.

"What you're saying is that I don't know my own mind. That I can't see what's in front of me and make my own decision. Is that it?"

"You don't know what you're getting into, though."

"Yes, I do. You've just told me. You need patience, and love, and someone in your life who will, for once, stand by you. Do you think I'm incapable of that?" Mirra demanded.

Silas's mouth dropped open. "It's just that –"

"Yes, I get it. You're broken. But you know what, Silas? All the best people are. Because broken people know how to treat people well. You know to show up. To be honest. To be ethical. To not lie. Your code of honor is so strong you could cut a diamond with it. You're a hard worker, you absolutely dote on Splash, and you're so desperate for love that you're blinded to it. All you have to do is let someone in."

"I don't know if I know how." Silas's look dropped to his hands, his voice cracking.

"Then I'll love you enough for the both of us, until you learn."

CHAPTER 25

Mirra pulled her dress over her head and Silas's mouth dropped open as she sauntered to the bed. She had a healthy appreciation of her body, so she was certain that Silas would enjoy her curves, and the look on his face reinforced her belief.

Stopping next to him, she picked up his hand and held it to her heart. "Thank you for sharing your past with me, Silas. You don't have to be lonely anymore if you don't want to be," Mirra whispered. "I love all your broken pieces. I love how they come together and form the most perfect man for me. Your willingness to be vulnerable with me only makes you stronger."

"I don't want to hurt you…" Silas breathed, his eyes caught on Mirra.

"You won't. Because you take care of the people you love." Mirra crawled onto the bed next to him and silenced his next words with a soft kiss. Just for a moment, she held his lips to her own, waiting for his resistance to soften. When it did, she drew back and met his eyes.

"I think you see me as something I'm not," Silas said.

"And I don't think you see yourself well enough." Mirra traced a finger over his lips.

"I haven't spent a lot of time looking," Silas admitted, pressing a kiss to her finger.

"A little self-reflection might do you some good. You're deserving of love, Silas. Beyond deserving. Won't you take what I offer?" Mirra whispered, her eyes holding his. She could see the storm in his eyes, and waited for the clouds to clear.

"I'd spend my life trying to live up to your love if you'd let me," Silas said.

Mirra closed her eyes as joy flooded through her. He was going to give her a chance.

"You have nothing to live up to," she said, leaning closer. "I just want you to be honest with your emotions. Just with me. Trust in me."

"It may take some time, but I'm willing to learn," Silas said, grinning at her, "if you're willing to be patient with me."

"Oh, I can be patient," Mirra said, then surprised Silas by rolling onto him and straddling his hips. He was still recovering, Mirra reminded herself, so she would need to take this slow and easy with him. "The question is…can you?"

"Mirra," Silas gasped as she bent forward and pressed soft kisses to his chest, then trailed her lips lower. "Wait. I want…"

"What do you want, Silas?" Mirra tilted her chin up to look at him from his waist.

"Kiss me."

Mirra slid her way gently up his body, careful not to rest her full weight on him, though she could feel how much he wanted her. Settling herself against his hardness, she bent and captured his lips with her mouth, moaning as he opened for her, toying with her tongue. Heat flushed through her, and a bone-deep knowledge that this person was her mate.

"I love the way you look at me," Mirra said, pulling back to see the raw hunger in Silas's eyes.

"I love the way you protected me from harm," she continued, kissing him once more before coming back up, gasping for air. Despite her best intentions, she found herself rubbing against his length, her body begging for more.

"I love the way you let a little dog become your best friend." She kissed down the side of his neck and ran her hands over the muscles of his chest. When she found his scar, she pressed the softest of kisses to the puckered skin.

"I love the way you look out for everyone else and take nothing for yourself." Mirra reached the waistband of Silas's shorts, and he groaned.

"Mirra...you're undoing me."

"I love how stubborn you are, even if it is infuriating at times." Mirra grinned when he swore. She tapped his hips and he lifted, allowing her to slide his shorts down his legs.

"I love how you devour books, how your mind is so eager to explore."

She bent and pressed a kiss to his length, laughing as he swore again, then taking him fully into her mouth. Enjoying her power, Mirra caressed him with her tongue, drawing out the pleasure until his hand threaded through her hair and he tugged her gently away.

"I can't…" Silas groaned.

"I love how you've fought for the life you wanted. And you made it happen," Mirra said, lazily stretching and kissing her way up his body before straddling him once more.

"Mirra…" His eyes were consumed with heat and something more – an emotion she hadn't seen there before. Love.

"And I love that you love me. Even if you don't fully understand it yet." Mirra paused to protect them both with a condom, before she bent to take his mouth once more as she lowered herself over him. They both moaned into each other's mouths, and soon they were lost in each other as passion overtook them, lust and love entwining to pull them both over the edge into exquisite bliss.

When they'd sated themselves, Mirra rolled to her side and made a move to get up. Silas's arm hooked around her and he pulled her back to him.

"Stay," Silas ordered.

"I will."

"No. I mean forever," Silas said, his voice already drifting into sleep. "Nobody stays with me. I want you to."

"I will. I promise."

But Silas had already fallen asleep. Mirra blinked back the sheen of tears that covered her eyes as she thought of the man beside her, his heart just aching for love.

Mirra eventually slipped from the bed and showered, and returned to find Silas awake and looking at her with a relaxed grin on his face. She'd never seen him so unguarded before, and her heart did a little dance in her chest.

"We need to talk," Silas said, patting the bed by him. Though nervousness slipped through Mirra, she crawled into bed and pulled the sheet over her body as Silas cradled her in.

"What's wrong?" Mirra asked, worry in her voice.

"We need to talk about what happened on the boat the other night," Silas said, his eyes searching hers. "I've had a few days to think things over."

"About Ronaldo? I'm so sorry. Was he your friend?"

"Yes, he was, but that's another conversation." Silas reached out and ran his finger across her cheek. "I saw you when I fell into the water."

"Did you?" Mirra asked, her eyes holding his. "What did you see?"

"You really are a mermaid, aren't you? Unless I've completely lost my mind."

"I believe I've already told you that I am," Mirra pointed out, waiting with bated breath.

"And I very rudely refused to believe you."

"And now?"

"I believe you," Silas said, shaking his head for a moment before bending over to press a kiss to her lips. "I'm sorry I didn't believe you when you told me. I'm sorry I thought you were lying to me. You have to understand how wild this is to me."

"Is it, though? You're a sailor. You enjoy reading about mermaids. You even have a mermaid tattoo," Mirra pointed out, tracing her finger over the tattoo on his arm. "One that looks just like me, mind you."

"I can see that," Silas said, looking down at his arm. "Maybe I manifested you."

"Oh, now you believe in manifesting too? What happened to the guy who only knows about hard work and a hard life?"

"Maybe I just needed to be shown a little magick." Silas smiled again, pulling Mirra tighter against him.

"Well, I'm glad you believe. It was a little insulting that you just thought I was delusional and were willing to put up with me being crazy."

"In all fairness, it's not exactly the most normal thing I've heard anyone say."

Mirra sniffed. "Well, I'm unique."

"You're more than unique. You're mind-blowing. I think you're incredible, Mirra, and I'm honored you've shared your secret with me. I promise to protect it – and you – with my life."

"I'm sure that won't be necessary, but I'm just happy you're willing to accept me."

"Did you think I wouldn't?" Silas brought his brow to hers.

"It was certainly a concern. Especially since you thought I was a nutjob. It's not…well, this life isn't for everyone, Silas. Not everyone can accept us for what we are."

"It's a gift," Silas decided. "It's truly a gift you've given me. You've opened my mind to so many other possibilities in this world. I'm going to have about a thousand questions for you, of course. And if you can accept me for who and what I am, there's no way I can't do the same for you. But, like, you know…my stuff is bad stuff and your stuff is brilliant and amazing and out of this world," Silas finished with a groan. "I'm making an ass of myself."

"No, I get it." Mirra laughed up at him, her heart full to bursting. "It's a lot to take in. And I think what you're trying to say is that we both have secret selves that we don't share with just anyone. So you're my person and I'm your person."

"You're more than just my person. You're my mermaid."

And then there was no more talking as Silas bent his head to Mirra and proceeded to worship her as the goddess she was.

CHAPTER 26

*A*s much as Silas had wanted to stay with Mirra and cocoon himself away from his responsibilities, duty called. The next day, Silas returned home for a quick change of clothes. Mirra dropped him off, and left him with a lingering kiss that seared straight to his core.

It humbled him, these feelings he had for her, and they were all tied up and knotted in his stomach like a big string of Christmas lights. He was hoping that, with a little space to breathe, he'd be able to sort these new emotions out and compartmentalize them so that they all made sense to him. But for now? He was a mess. After giving it some thought, though, Silas found that he didn't mind being a mess. Which was also something new for him, he mused.

Good sex would do that to a person.

At least that was what he was trying to tell himself, Silas thought as he drove into work. For someone who'd just been shot, he was surprisingly cheerful. He didn't mind the emotions buzzing about within, he didn't care that he would have a scar from the bullet wound, and last but not least he didn't mind if anyone thought he was crazy.

He was going to marry Mirra.

That was the only thought front and center in his mind. He just had to figure out how to convince her. If being with her made him feel this good, he'd take a chance that she'd stay true to her word and help him sort out all this emotional stuff he still wasn't quite sure of.

But first, he needed to deal with the captain and write up his report. His stomach sank as he thought about his friend and brother, Ronaldo. The man had looked at him like Silas had meant nothing to him. He still couldn't believe that he'd been so wrong about a person. It wasn't often that his instincts were wrong, but they'd missed the mark by a mile with Ronaldo.

Worry poked at him. Could he trust his own intuition with Mirra? Maybe he needed to pump the brakes there too; to take a moment before he rushed into anything. Maybe he was just on a high after almost dying. Now more than a little confused, Silas pulled into his parking spot and sat for a moment as his thoughts bounced around like ping-pong balls.

Finally, when he couldn't come to a solid conclusion, Silas sighed and left the truck. Splash had insisted on staying at the Laughing Mermaid, and since Silas knew they doted on him, he'd let the dog have a few days off from work.

The captain's door was partially open. "Captain Reid?" Silas knocked and ducked his head in the door.

"Silas!" Captain Reid sprang up from his chair, dropping the papers he held in his hand and rounding the desk.

Before Silas could dodge him, the captain engulfed him in a big bear hug, slapping him heartily on the back. "Oh, shoot, I'm sorry. I know you're injured. Come in, come in."

"It's okay," Silas said, rubbing unconsciously at the scar at his chest. "I'm healing up." He was surprised at the captain's display of affection though. The Marine Enforcement was known to be a tight-knit group, but they weren't particularly touchy.

"Sit, sit. Can I get you a coffee?" The captain stopped by the pot on his sideboard; it was always full.

"Sure, thanks."

"I can't tell you how happy I am to see you up and about. We had ourselves a pretty scary time there, thinking you were lost." The captain turned, his eyebrows raised in question as he handed Silas coffee in a mug with a pink flamingo on it. Likely from his daughter, Silas thought. She had a penchant for finding outrageous mugs for her father to take to work.

"I can imagine. It was pretty scary for me too." He and Mirra had discussed how to answer the questions that were sure to come his way, as he had disappeared from the area where the boats had been. They'd settled on a solution that they thought would make the most sense, and they had the necessary witnesses to back it up if need be.

"Can you tell me what happened? You know I still need to file an official report."

"Yes, I can. But first…what about Ronaldo? Did you get him?"

The captain looked at him in shock. "Nobody told you? I thought you'd been informed of the latest."

"No. I've been kind of out of it," Silas admitted.

"I'm sure you were. Well, when we boarded your boat, he was neatly tied up and ready for us to take in. His eyes were wide and he was babbling about mermaids. Almost like he was having some sort of hallucination. I couldn't get a word of sense out of him, and we have him sitting in jail now, waiting on international extradition to Colombia."

"I..." Silas's voice trailed off. He had no idea what to say or think about that. If Mirra had been busy saving his life, that meant *other* mermaids had stepped in to help him – likely Jolie and Irma. Mirra's family.

His family, Silas realized. An emotion he had never felt flooded through him, warming him all the way down to his toes. They hadn't even known if he would accept Mirra or be in a relationship with her, yet they'd still put themselves on the line to protect him. Family, Silas thought again with a small smile, and shook his head in wonder.

"Something funny?"

"I just... I can't even make heads or tails of it, Cap. I'm trying to think how something like that could have happened," Silas looked up and met the captain's eyes. He took a sip of the black coffee and relaxed back into his chair as the first hit of caffeine flooded him.

"It's pretty strange. The only thing we could think is that maybe one of the cartel members considered him a liability and circled back. Maybe drugged him so he was ranting and raving by the time we showed up."

"That would make sense." Silas nodded and took

another sip of coffee, studiously ignoring the captain's look.

They both knew that if the cartel had truly considered someone a liability, then they would have shot them. Dead men tell no tales, after all...

The captain shook his head and reached for his recorder. "Your report?" Turning the machine on, he waved to Silas.

"It all happened really fast..."

Silas gave all the details of the report – at least, all the details he felt comfortable giving. He left out the fact that the barrels had been pulled away in the darkness and he certainly wasn't going to say anything about seeing Mirra when he hit the water. "And then he fired on me. I had already started to throw myself backwards overboard, so my foot caught the gun. I imagine that's the only thing that saved me."

"That's a lot of blood in the water, though. I'm surprised you didn't attract sharks." The captain studied him over his own mug of coffee.

"So am I. I'm lucky. There's nothing else to say about it. I'm damn lucky."

"And this Lucas fellow found you? Pulled you into his dinghy, I heard?"

"How did you hear that?" Silas asked.

"Small island. You know how it goes. I'm grateful he found you."

"As am I. And I'm damn lucky the ladies at the Laughing Mermaid had a surgeon staying with them this week. It sounds like I would have been in rough shape if I'd tried to make it to the hospital."

"Yes, I imagine you owe them quite a debt."

"Captain…" Silas nodded to the recorder, and the captain interpreted his intention correctly and shut it off. "I owe you an apology."

"For what?" The captain leaned back in his chair and crossed his arms over his chest.

"I didn't know Ronaldo was a traitor. I should've figured it out. I knew there was *someone*, and…well, for a brief moment I worried it was you. When Splash got stolen, I couldn't figure out why you'd taken him for a walk. I thought maybe…just for a moment…" Silas couldn't bring himself to say it. Instead he looked shamefully down at the mug of coffee in his hands.

"You thought it was me."

"I wondered. I thought something was up. But looking back, I see now that it was Ronaldo. He ran back that night – to grab his radio, he said – and I kept on going."

"You don't owe me an apology. I'm glad you questioned me. Your instincts were right to question anything that didn't make sense. We did have a traitor on our hands. I wouldn't have trained you well if you hadn't thought to question me. I take no offense."

"Seriously?"

"Of course. The only thing I'm upset about is Ronaldo. Damn it." The captain leaned forward and pounded a fist on the desk. "I really liked him."

"I did too. I considered him a friend. I'd been to his family's house for dinner."

"His wife is a sweetheart. I worry for them now."

"He said he did it for money. The family was in debt

back in Colombia. Perhaps he was driven to it because he felt he had no option."

"We all make choices, Silas. He could have come to me for money. I would have helped him. Hell, all of us would have pitched in to help him. There's always another way. He chose the wrong side. It's not on us to decide what happens next."

"Can we do something for the family at least?" Silas knew what it was like to suddenly be rudderless, and he was sure Ronaldo's wife was feeling that way right now.

"I've already set it up. We'll get together a fundraiser to help with some of the bills."

"You're a good man, Captain."

"As are you, Silas. I'm proud to have you on the team. And I mean that from the bottom of my heart." The captain met his eye and they shared a manly-type moment, acknowledging their feelings for each other without saying anything more.

The captain cleared his throat. "So, do I hear that you and Mirra...?"

"Yes. In fact, I have a favor to ask of you."

"Consider it done."

"Perfect, because I think I want to move fast on this. When's your next night off work?"

"I can take any night off work. It depends on what you need me for."

"I need you for sunset. On one of the boats."

"You've got it. When?"

"Tomorrow?" Silas's heart jumped as he thought about it. But he needed to move fast or he'd lose his nerve.

"As I said, consider it done."

"Perfect. Here's what I'm thinking…"

By the time Silas was walking back to his car, his stomach was back in knots and he'd left the captain with a mile-wide smile on his face. He had one more stop to make, then he'd just have to throw a few plans in motion without Mirra being any the wiser.

Moments later, Silas's truck rolled to a stop in front of Prince's house. Luck seemed to be on his side today, and he found Prince in his garden, machete in hand.

"I come in peace," Silas called, throwing his hands in the air.

"Peace is de best way, man. But a machete is good to have around, eh?" Prince grinned his gap-toothed smile at Silas. "You lookin' good for somebody done took a bullet."

"I am good." Silas rubbed his scar again. He wondered if he would always do that now whenever someone mentioned him being shot. "I need your help."

"Dat sounds interesting. Come in, come in." Prince waved him in with the machete. "You want a drink?"

"I just had a coffee. I'm good. Prince…I have a few questions for you."

"Go on." Prince plopped into a chair and stretched legs clad in faded shorts out in front of him. The wind rustled the palms quietly, and Prince took a sip of his coconut. Wiping the back of his hand across his face, he smiled again.

"You believe in mermaids, don't you?"

"Of course. I tol' you dat, don't I?"

"Yes, I think you did at one time."

"You seen one?" Prince gestured with his coconut.

"Yes, I've seen one," Silas admitted quietly. He didn't think he was betraying anyone's trust by speaking to Prince about this, but he waited to see what the man would say.

"'Bout time she showed herself to you. Mirra trusts you den."

"Why do you say it's her?" Silas squinted, feigning a look of confusion.

"Because she likes you. I was wondering when she'd tell you."

"I want to marry her." Silas decided not to say anything about Mirra until he'd confirmed with her that Prince knew about their history.

"As you should! She's de best of dem, I swear she is. Actually, all women are de best women. But Mirra, ah. She just touches my soul." Prince kissed his fingers to his lips.

"She's a rare woman," Silas agreed, "which is why I need your help. You did such a good job with that pearl I found – I'm wondering if you can help me out."

"You want a ring?" Prince sat up in excitement.

"I want a ring. But I want it for tomorrow. I need to move fast on this or I'll do something stupid, like talk myself out of it and list all the reasons why I'm not worthy of her or why she should be with someone else. For some damn reason, she's picked me. I'd be a fool to pass her up."

"You would be a fool. I'm glad you're not. Now. I know just de ting for her."

"You do?"

"Sure, sure. Prince knows everything. Come with me,

man. We've got to call my Maria. She'll make dis happen."

"Thanks, Prince. I really appreciate the help."

"No problem, man. We family here." Prince slapped him on the back and Silas found himself grinning. Maybe, just maybe, he'd had family all along if he'd only allowed himself to see it.

Siren Island really *was* his home.

CHAPTER 27

"Is that what you're going to wear?" Jolie raised an eyebrow at Mirra as she came into Mirra's bedroom unannounced, like sisters everywhere did.

"Thanks for knocking."

"Like you ever knock when you come into my room."

"Now that you're with Ted, I do."

"Good point. Except we never do that here. And I know Silas isn't with you, because you're going to meet him for your first date. Therefore, no need to knock."

"I find you very annoying," Mirra decided, studying herself in her mirror. "What's wrong with this? We're going on the boat." She'd pulled on a pair of cute cut-off jean shorts and wore a lacy red tank. It was casual and sexy, and struck just the right notes for a sunset boat ride.

"Ugh, you only get one first date, Mirra. Have I taught you nothing?" Jolie disappeared into the closet, and Mirra soon heard the sound of hangers being shoved about.

"You always liked to dress up more than I did anyhow. I'm much simpler."

"There's simple and there's...*that*." Jolie poked her head out and gave Mirra a disapproving look. Mirra threw up her hands and plopped down onto the bed, knowing there wasn't going to be much she could do to dissuade Jolie once her sister got in this mood. Plus, Jolie really did have good taste, so she submitted to the inevitable.

"Seriously, I need to revamp your closet," Jolie said. "I can't believe it's been this long since I've done a clean-out. Be right back."

Jolie stomped from the room and Mirra just shook her head in wonder at the empty space. It wasn't like her style was *that* bad. It seemed Jolie was even more nervous about Mirra's first date than Mirra was herself.

When Jolie returned, her arms brimming with dresses, Mirra laughed. "What in the world, Jolie? I have plenty of nice stuff."

"But you don't want just nice. You want wow, you know?" Jolie dropped the dresses on the bed.

"Jolie. The man's already seen all my wow." Mirra laughed. "I don't think he'll much care what I wear."

"It's your first date and I'm making you look perfect, the end." Jolie pushed her lower lip out stubbornly, and Mirra threw up her hands. There really was no use arguing once that lip came out.

"Fine. Do your best."

"Great! Okay, so I raided Mom's closet since most of my stuff isn't here anymore." Jolie hummed as she dug through the pile of dresses, holding up and discarding them so fast that Mirra barely got a chance to say anything. Then her eye caught on an ombre-looking one.

"Oh...what's that?"

"Ohhh, this might be a good choice. Yes." Jolie nodded her head and held up the dress. It was cut low in a halter style that left the back bare. The silk flowed to the floor in cascading hue of blues, looking like the ocean as it grew deeper. The straps tied in a bow around the neck, but the cleavage wasn't cut so deeply as to be scandalous. All in all it was extremely sexy yet delightfully elegant.

"This seems a little fancy for a boat ride."

"Do you care?" Jolie met her eyes.

"Actually, no. I love it. Let me try it on." Jolie was right. Mirra did want to feel beautiful for their first real date. She smiled at the memory of Silas calling her up and politely asking her to accompany him for a sunset cruise. He'd told her that it was important to him that he properly court her, and that this would mark the first official date of the rest of their lives together. She'd laughed at that, but he'd charmed her with his willingness to see a future for them as a couple. It was like a switch had flipped in Silas, and she was more than excited that he was taking their future seriously.

"It's a full moon tonight, you know," Jolie called as Mirra slipped the dress over her head in the bathroom. She'd taken her bra off, as it wouldn't be possible to wear one in this dress, and shivered as the cool silk settled over her body.

"I did know that. Hopefully we'll be on the boat long enough to watch the moon rise."

"Come out here," Jolie demanded. Mirra did, stopping before the full-length mirror.

"Oh, Jolie!" Mirra gasped, holding her hand to her mouth. Her sister came and stood behind her, resting her head on Mirra's shoulder. Her twin. Dark to her light. "This is really beautiful. Is this yours or Mom's?"

"It's Mom's. She thought it would be perfect for you."

"It is." The blues worked well with Mirra's cool blond coloring, and the dress rippled over her curves like water.

"Here, let me do your hair." Jolie tugged her to the bathroom and began to do a complicated series of braids and twists. She stopped and wandered back to Mirra's jewelry box, then returned to the bathroom to tuck a few pins into her sister's hair. "There. What do you think?"

"It's perfect," Mirra breathed. Jolie had braided and twisted her hair back from her crown and left the rest to tumble down Mirra's back in a riot of waves. The pins she'd tucked into Mirra's hair had pearls on them, and they were all the ornamentation she needed.

"No jewelry. Then you'd look too fancy."

"You're right. This is just right." Mirra touched a pearl. "A little bit of luster, a really sexy dress, and nothing else."

"Silas is going to swallow his tongue."

"That's the plan." Mirra laughed, giddiness flooding her. "I'm just so happy, Jolie. I was worried he wasn't going to accept me."

"He'd be a damn fool not to."

"You know what I mean. We're not for everyone."

"Which is why Silas is your mate and not anyone else." Jolie checked a slim watch at her wrist. "And you, my dear, had better run or you're going to miss the sunset."

"Oh shoot, is it that late already?"

"He's been here for like fifteen minutes already, at least."

"He's here?" Mirra shot Jolie an enraged look. "And you're just telling me this now?"

"Yes. It's good to make him wait. Plus, look how good you look. You'll thank me later, I promise."

"Yeah, yeah. Whatever." Mirra glared at her and grabbed a small purse before bounding out the door.

She skidded to a stop when she heard Silas's voice. Feeling a bit shy now, she took a few deep breaths before walking forward.

Irma turned to look at her from the front door, where she was talking with Silas. "Oh, Mirra. You look lovely," she said, beaming at her.

True to Jolie's promise, Silas turned and his mouth dropped open. He stood like that for a moment, nothing coming out.

"Told ya," Jolie whispered from back in the hallway.

"Shut it," Mirra hissed over her shoulder before turning back and smiling at Silas. "Hello, Silas."

"You look like an angel." Silas bent and pressed a kiss to her cheek. Was the man trembling? Surprised, Mirra reached up and pressed a hand to his cheek.

"Thank you. You look very handsome yourself." It was the first time she'd seen Silas in anything other than a work uniform or board shorts. Tonight he'd put on linen khaki pants, and wore a lightweight white short-sleeve button-down shirt which only highlighted his tan and the sexy tattoos running down his arms.

"No shoes, Mirra?" Irma laughed.

"Oh, shoot." Mirra tried to turn around, but Silas kept her hand.

"You won't need them."

The air escaped her when he swept her up into his arms and carried her to his truck, to a round of applause from Jolie and Irma.

"Oh, well now you've really given them something to talk about," Mirra laughed.

"I've been known to be romantic a time or two in my life," Silas said as he opened the door and gently put her on the front seat. Mirra had never been one to fall for obvious romantic gestures, and yet her heart fluttered in her chest at his moves.

"I hope I'm not overdressed." Mirra smoothed her skirt. "Jolie bulldozed me into changing. She's a force of nature at times."

"I'm glad she did. You look ravishing in anything you wear, but this is really spectacular. Perfect for our first date."

They chatted easily on the way into town and Mirra laughed again when Silas insisted on carrying her to the boat once they'd arrived at the harbor.

"I could get used to this," Mirra decided, her arms around Silas's neck.

"I would have no problem carrying you everywhere for the rest of my life," Silas said, his tone serious. "Not to mention that I love how you feel in my arms."

"I like your arms around me too," Mirra said, surprised to feel a blush rising on her cheeks. There was something about being carried in Silas's muscular arms that was making her feel dainty and ladylike, though she knew she ran more to curvaceous and headstrong.

"Here we are," Silas said, stepping easily onto the back of his boat, still carrying Mirra. She smiled as he slid her slowly down his body. Tilting her head up, her smile grew wider when he leaned down to brush a soft kiss over her lips. When someone cleared their throat behind them, Mirra jumped back.

"Captain Reid!" Mirra laughed in embarrassed relief, and then laughed harder when Splash ran over to her. "Does he have a bowtie on?"

"Of course. We're all putting on our finest for our big date tonight," Silas said.

"I'll be your captain this evening so Silas may enjoy the sunset with you." Captain Reid swept his hand out and ushered Mirra to a seat on the side of the boat. "If you'll just take a seat here, we'll be on our way shortly."

"Of course."

Mirra smiled as Splash plopped himself at her feet, and she watched as the men worked seamlessly to untie the boat and motor them out of the harbor. She didn't mind that the Captain was here, though she had hoped for some alone time with Silas. Plenty of time for that, Mirra reminded herself, and settled in to enjoy the breeze on her face as the sun began to kiss the horizon. Warm rays of yellow and pink flowed across the water and danced over a few wisps of clouds hanging low in the sky. Mirra hummed to herself as the boat raced across the ocean. They were heading to the north of the island, near the Laughing Mermaid, and she wondered if she'd be able to wave to her family from the water if they were out in the garden.

When the motor cut, Mirra looked up. "Are we stopping?"

"Yes. This is a nice spot to watch the sunset."

Mirra decided not to point out that they were virtually in front of her house and they could have watched it from there. This was his date and she was letting him be in control.

"Will you join me at the front of the boat, my lady?" Silas bowed before her and Mirra laughed.

"Why, yes, good sir, I'd be delighted to." Mirra stood and took his arm. He escorted her past the captain's chair and through a small passageway to the front of the boat. Once there, she skidded to a stop. "Oh, Silas."

Fairy lights had been strung across the bow of the boat to form a sweeping archway, and flowers were scattered all across the deck. The sun's late-afternoon rays cast their glow across the scene, and Mirra had to blink back tears at the beauty of it. When she turned to him, she gasped and held her hand to her mouth.

Silas was down on one knee.

"Mirra, I…" Silas took a deep breath, steadying his voice, and met her eyes. "I didn't know, before I met you, that I could ever understand what love is. I think I'm still wrapping my head around it all. But what I do know, more than anything else, is that I can't take a breath without thinking of you. My life was on autopilot before I met you and I was certain I was content. But now I realize I was just drifting along, stuck in a holding pattern. I don't want to drift anymore, Mirra. I want to swim with the mermaids. Will you do me the honor of becoming my wife?"

"Oh, yes, Silas. I absolutely will!" Mirra blinked back the tears that flooded her eyes. She was glad she had opted for the no-makeup look as she sniffed, trying to control the emotion that flooded her.

Silas stood and presented her with a ring.

"May I?" Silas whispered.

"Yes." Mirra blinked down at the ring he slid on her finger. It fit as if it were made for her, and she could feel the love pulsing from the ring as it warmed her palm. It was an oval aquamarine stone, shining in a lovely shade of pale blue, surrounded by diamonds set in a floral filigree rose-gold band. It was everything – earth and ocean and the sunset combined. He'd picked the perfect ring for her. "Oh, Silas, this is beautiful."

"Do you like it? I was so worried you'd hate it."

"No, it's perfect," Mirra promised him.

"I love you, Mirra." It was the first time he'd said it, and Mirra's heart swelled with joy. "I know I'm a work in progress, but I will spend my life making you happy."

"I love you too, Silas. I'd be honored to be your wife."

"I hope you mean that, because I have one other big thing to ask of you."

"Okay…" Mirra blew out a breath. "Hit me with it."

"I'd like for you to marry me."

Mirra laughed at him. "You already asked me that."

"I mean, right now. Here."

"Now?" Mirra gaped at him, and then looked at the fairy lights dancing over their heads and the flowers scattered across the deck. "Why now?"

"I'm scared I'll do something stupid and talk myself out of the best thing that's ever happened to me. But I need you to be sure."

"I'm sure, Silas. Yes, I'll marry you today. Tomorrow. Whenever." Mirra laughed.

"I can't tell you how happy that makes me." A grin lit

Silas's face. Turning, he ducked his head in the door to the driver's area. "Captain! She said yes. You're up."

Mirra laughed again as the captain walked through the door and positioned himself at the front of the boat. He'd changed into a suit coat and held a little book in his hands. Splash followed and sat at his feet, looking resplendent in his bowtie. The sun had dipped below the horizon and the last pinky streaks tinted the sky.

"Look!" Mirra pointed to where the moon, a huge golden orb, was rising from the depths of the dark water. "Oh, it's just the perfect moon for tonight."

"Then shall we?" Silas asked. He offered her his arm, and they took two small steps forward to stand before the captain.

"It is my honor – and I mean that from the very depths of my heart – to be here today to officiate your wedding. As a captain, I've always had the authority to officiate at weddings, but never have I been as honored as I am today to marry a man I love like a son and a woman for whom I hold nothing but the highest regard."

Mirra glanced at Silas to see him dash the back of his hand across his eyes. She knew what it meant to him to have Captain here, to have someone who was as close to him as family could be. She swallowed past the lump in her throat.

"Today, I'm honored to bring together two souls whose love, though new and bright and shiny, will only grow more lovely with age," the captain began, and Mirra felt love just pour through her at the thought that she was getting everything she'd ever wanted.

"Silas, would you like to say something?" Captain nodded to Silas.

He turned to Mirra and grasped her hands, looking down at her as the boat swayed gently beneath them and the moon rose over their heads.

"Thank you for seeing me for who I am, Mirra. I've always thought that I was broken and that I'd never be whole. But now I realize I wasn't broken – I was just missing a piece. That piece is you, Mirra. With you, I'm whole and I'm ready to take on the world, so long as you are at my side. You make me believe in love again, in family, in loving good nights and happy good mornings. It's like you've shined your light into the darkest crevices of my being and showed me that I had nothing to be scared of all along. I was just waiting for you. I'm honored to be your husband and I will love you until my dying breath."

Mirra blinked back tears and leaned forward to kiss Silas before Captain interrupted her. "Not yet, Mirra."

"Oh, right." Mirra laughed. "Silas, I've known since the moment you risked your life to save me that you were the man for me. Fearless, selfless, and with a heart that just needed to trust in love. You're going to be the solid base to my whimsy, the foundation to my heart, and the anchor to my boat. You steady me and I trust you to help navigate our future together. As a family."

Silas squeezed her hands tightly as they both turned to the captain.

"Silas, do you take Mirra to be your beautiful wife?"

"I do." Silas beamed at her.

"Mirra, do you take Silas to be your steadfast husband?"

"I do," Mirra whispered.

"Then it is with absolute joy that, by the power vested in me, I now pronounce you husband and wife. You may kiss the bride." Captain beamed at them and gestured with his hands, stepping back as Silas took Mirra in his arms.

He took her breath away, his love pouring through her and warming her to her core. A loud cheer tore her away from Silas, and they both turned to the shore. Tiki torches lit the beach there, and a large group of people could be seen gathered around a bonfire dancing and cheering. Mirra laughed when Splash threw his head back and howled.

"You told everyone?" Mirra blinked up at Silas.

"That, my dear, is our wedding party. Shall we join the festivities?"

"Oh, I was – well, I was so happy, but I was wishing Jolie and my mother could be here. And they were!" Mirra wiped tears from her eyes as the captain resumed his seat at the steering wheel and started the engine.

"Shall we go join our party?" Silas leaned down and kissed her again. "My wife."

"Yes, my love, we shall." The boat drove into the path of the moonlight glowing across the water. Mirra gasped as dolphins began to leap from the water, one by one, until hundreds of them charioted the boat home.

CHAPTER 28

*S*he couldn't have planned it better if she'd done it herself, Mirra decided, as she and Silas danced down the garden path to the beach. Splash raced ahead to be greeted by Snowy and Pipin, both of whom also sported bowties. Mirra couldn't stop laughing and crying at the same time as Jolie and Irma ran out of the crowd to throw their arms around the two of them.

"It was perfect," Jolie squealed.

"Absolutely stunning. You did fantastic, Silas."

"I wished you could have been there. And then, you were!" Mirra laughed.

"Lucas had his drone up, so we even got video for you." Samantha, who lived next door with Lucas, stepped forward to hug Mirra.

"He did? Oh, that's – I'm so happy," Mirra exclaimed, hugging her back. "That's fantastic news. I didn't even think about pictures. It all just happened so fast." Mirra jumped as Prince appeared and popped a bottle of champagne.

"Congratulations, sweet mermaid. You deserve all de happiness in de world." Prince pressed a kiss to her cheek and handed them both flutes of champagne before dancing away with the bottle in his hand.

"Let me see the ring," Jolie demanded, and grabbed Mirra's hand. "Oh, aquamarine. It's perfect."

"It really is. How did you know?" Mirra glanced up at Silas.

"Prince helped me. He seems to know everything about everyone. He said you wouldn't mind that it wasn't a diamond center-stone."

"I don't. Aquamarine is perfect for me."

"Good. I'm happy you like it."

"Oh." Mirra cast a stricken look at Silas. "I don't have a ring for you. I didn't know…"

"It's okay, my love. I knew you wouldn't. We'll pick one out together," Silas said, and pressed a kiss to her cheek. Together they drifted over to the group that swayed to the music by the bonfire. A long table held platters of food, and a bouncy reggae beat pulsed from the speakers set up in the corner. Mirra looked around to see all of the people she loved smiling back at her.

She pitched her voice above the music. "I'd like to thank everyone for coming to my surprise wedding. If you'd all raise your glasses?"

The crowd raised their glasses and Mirra turned to Silas. "To exploring new depths…together."

The crowd cheered and they all drank, Mirra continuing to blink back the tears she was having trouble keeping away. It had been a whirlwind few weeks since she'd first tried to save the dolphins, and now here she was stepping into her future with a man about whom she still had so much to learn. And yet, she wasn't afraid. She knew that no matter what troubles came their way, they'd weather the storm together.

"Mirra." Irma beckoned from the shadows, and Mirra squeezed Silas's hand before slipping away to go to her mother.

Jolie quickly joined them. "What are you all hiding away over here for?" she immediately demanded.

"Not that you were invited, but I'm glad you came over as well." Irma shot Jolie a look, but her daughter only grinned at her. Jolie looked smashing in a flowing red dress, her dark curls tumbling about her head.

"Always good to know I'm welcome." Jolie fluttered her lashes at Irma.

"Mirra, love, are you happy?" Irma asked, her eyes searching Mirra's. She knew how her mother worried for her.

"Yes. I am. Truly. I know it seems like such a whirlwind, but it just feels right. I have no regrets and I truly look forward to our future together. I trust that he's a good man and he'll try to make me happy."

"He's a man who doesn't love easily. But when he does – that's it. He's done for. You'll never have to worry about him with other women or any such issues. He'll only have eyes for you. That kind of love matters. I couldn't be happier for you." Irma held out her hand. "So, with Jolie's permission, of course, I'll give you this."

"What is this?" Jolie demanded, leaning over to look into Irma's palm. A simple hammered-gold band glinted in the moonlight.

"This was a ring from your father's family. I was going to offer it to whomever married first. I only have this one ring, so you both will need to decide if you are comfortable with Mirra having it."

"Mirra should take it," Jolie said immediately.

"Oh, Jolie. Are you sure? You'll be married soon. You could have it for Ted."

"No, it's perfect. You didn't know you were getting married and this ring is here for you to use. You can just feel the love around it, can't you? Plus, you know I'm not as sentimental as you. It will mean more to you."

"Are you sure?" Mirra asked once more as she took the ring gently from Irma's palm.

"I'm sure. I'm just so happy for you, Mirra."

"Are *you* sure?" Mirra looked at her mother with compassion. "This is… I mean, this is all you have of him." Mirra held it up so that the firelight danced over the gold.

"You're wrong." Irma smiled softly. "I have my memories of him. It's meant to be worn, not hidden in a box somewhere. I'd like to know it will be worn with love."

"I'll take it, then. Thank you." Mirra reached out and wrapped her arms around Irma, leaning into her mother and holding her for a moment. Jolie's arms came around them both, and together the three of them swayed gently, their love uniting them.

"Now, I do believe it's time to party, isn't it?" Irma stepped back and laughed, wiping her eyes. "I can't sit in the corner and cry all night."

"Let me find Silas and give him his ring. He'll be so surprised!" Mirra bounced across the sand, the ring pulsing gently in her pocket, until she found Silas talking to Prince and Maria.

"There she is." Maria, a round dark woman who was the true love of Prince's life, beamed up at her. "Congratulations, my love."

"Thank you. I heard you helped with the ring. It's perfect, truly." Mirra held out her hand so that the firelight caught the stones of her ring, making it glitter.

"I knew de aquamarine was perfect for you."

"And I have something perfect for you." Mirra turned to Silas and held up the golden ring. "This was my father's ring. I'd like for you to have it."

"Are you…are you sure?" Silas's eyes filled with awe as he looked down at her. "Your mother won't mind?"

"No. She wants you to have it."

"It's nice. Dis a nice gesture, isn't it?" Prince beamed, then rolled his eyes when Maria tsked and dragged him away so Mirra and Silas could have a moment alone.

"Here. Let's see." With a smile, Mirra took Silas's hand. When the ring slipped easily onto his finger, he gaped down at it and then at her.

"It fits perfectly."

"It was meant to be," Mirra decided.

Silas held up his hand and tested the weight of it. "It feels good. Warm against my hand. Like there's love there."

"You feel it?" Mirra's smile widened.

"I do, actually."

"Then it's even more perfect." Mirra tilted her head up for his kiss, and then leaned into him when he put his arm around her shoulders. Turning, they looked at the small crowd on the beach.

"This is your family now, Silas."

"It is. You've been here all along. I just had to see it."

"In that case, welcome home."

IRMA SLIPPED AWAY from the group and wandered down the beach, taking a moment to herself. Her heart was filled to bursting with love and happiness for her children. She'd watched as Mirra had slipped the ring on Silas, and seen how he'd all but glowed with love for her. It had been the right choice, giving Mirra that ring for Silas. The man cried out for the love of family, and she was going to enjoy making up for lost time with all the mothering she planned to do for him.

But still…her heart had twinged a bit when she'd handed the ring over. Not because she begrudged Mirra her happiness. No, not that at all. It was just that Irma had only had such a short chance at a love like that. She missed her love…but more than anything she missed giving her love to a partner. She hadn't lied to Mirra when she'd said that she was capable of living a rich and fulfilling life without a partner at her side. But there was a part of her that ached to feel that love once more.

Looking out to where the moon cast its light over the dark waves, Irma dared to make a wish – a wish she'd never made before. Whispering it on the wind, she let the moment draw out…then she turned her back on the moon and returned to the beach where her loved ones danced beneath the stars.

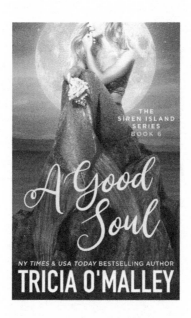

Available now!

**The following is a sneak peak from
A Good Soul**

Book 6 in the Siren Island Series

CHAPTER 1

*I*rma swam deep, pushing against the angst that twisted low in her gut. She hated this time of year, when storms rolled in and sailors were put at risk. Every summer, she relived the most catastrophic moment of her life – and she would continue to do so. Even if it had only saved one life, it would still be worth it.

She hadn't been able to save them all. For that, Irma felt genuine regret. But, as she often reminded herself, she was only one woman – only one mermaid – and she could only do so much.

The sea churned at the surface, the storm rolling in, and Irma swam deeper so that the pull of the waves wouldn't interfere with her direction. In her mermaid form, she was strong – much stronger than in her human form – and she was able to cut easily through the angry sea as the storm rolled in overhead.

Her destination was the same as it had always been. The rocks where, what seemed like a lifetime ago now,

Nalachi had destroyed his boat – a place where Irma was determined to protect others from meeting the same fate. A reef system lived close to the surface there, and it was virtually undetectable when a storm was raging.

It had been her worst day, finding his boat wrecked on the rocks, Nalachi himself gasping for breath. She'd had her babies in tow, and they'd watched as their father had died. Having recently given birth, Irma's magick had been spent, and there'd been little she could do for Nalachi as the storm had all but swallowed them whole.

She'd taken care of his soul, protecting it the best she could and removing it to the Cave of Souls. Then she'd dived deep, taking her babies to live with her in the mermaid village far below the surface of the ocean. Her grief had threatened to consume her. Time passed far more slowly there than it did above the water, and the mermaids had nurtured Irma until she'd been ready to leave the safety of the village and take her babies to land.

When she returned to the island, many decades had passed, and Irma made the decision to raise her children on land. She didn't want to turn her back on the mermaid world, but she felt her children deserved the option of living a human life if they so chose. And so the Laughing Mermaid had been born, and she'd spent the last several years learning to live a different life.

She'd found joy on land, and had learned to enjoy the best of both worlds. It was only during the season of storms that her grief returned, and Irma had learned to live with it as best she could.

Now she surfaced near the rocks. Irma climbed up to

her safe spot, the rock she always secured herself on, and she began to sing.

Her grief rang out across the water, warning storm-addled boats away, as Irma paid her penance to her long-lost love.

Available for Pre-order now!

AFTERWORD

Unsurprisingly, I spend a lot of time underwater because I moved to the Caribbean to do just that. I have a very deep love for scuba-diving, and when I'm not writing I like to disappear into the ocean to take joy in the beauty that can be found there. I'm passionate about the conservation of coral reefs, and I love sharing this passion with my readers – both through my books and my scuba-diving photos that I share. I think a part of me has always dreamed of being a mermaid, as being underwater is a soothing and meditative experience for me. I hope my love for the ocean, my belief in the mystical, and my hope that fairy tales really can come true rings through for you in my books. Thanks for taking a peek into my world with me.

If you enjoy looking at scuba-diving photos, island pictures, puppy photos, and the occasional pictures of a hot Scotsman – be sure to sign up for my newsletter at www.-triciaomalley.com

Thanks for reading my story that I so lovingly put out into the world. I hope it brought you light and joy! If you can, I'd be honored if you left a review. A book can live and die by reviews and I so very much want my book to live. (Please don't kill my book!)

THE SIREN ISLAND SERIES

ALSO BY TRICIA O'MALLEY

Good Girl

Up to No Good

A Good Chance

Good Moon Rising

Too Good to Be True

A Good Soul

In Good Time

A completed series.

Available in audio, e-book & paperback!

"Love her books and was excited for a totally new and different one! Once again, she did NOT disappoint! Magical in multiple ways and on multiple levels. Her writing style, while similar to that of Nora Roberts, kicks it up a notch!! I want to visit that island, stay in the B&B and meet the gals who run it! The characters are THAT real!!!" - Amazon Review

WILD SCOTTISH KNIGHT

BOOK 1 IN THE ENCHANTED HIGHLANDS SERIES

Opposites attract in this modern-day fairytale when American, Sophie MacKnight, inherits a Scottish castle along with a hot grumpy Scotsman who is tasked with training her to be a magickal knight to save the people of Loren Brae.

A brand new series from Tricia O'Malley.
Wild Scottish Knight

THE WILDSONG SERIES

ALSO BY TRICIA O'MALLEY

Song of the Fae

Melody of Flame

Chorus of Ashes

Lyric of Wind

"The magic of Fae is so believable. I read these books in one sitting and can't wait for the next one. These are books you will reread many times."

- Amazon Review

Available in audio, e-book & paperback!

Available Now

THE ISLE OF DESTINY SERIES

ALSO BY TRICIA O'MALLEY

Do you want to learn more about how Bianca & Seamus fell in love and helped battle the Dark Fae during the Four Treasures quest? Read the complete Isle of Destiny series in Kindle Unlimited!

Stone Song

Sword Song

Spear Song

Sphere Song

A completed series.

Available in audio, e-book & paperback!

"Love this series. I will read this multiple times. Keeps you on the edge of your seat. It has action, excitement and romance all in one series."

- Amazon Review

"Not my usual genre but couldn't resist the Florida Keys setting. I was hooked from the first page. A fun read with just the right amount of crazy! Will definitely follow this series."- Amazon Review

A completed series.

Available in audio, e-book & paperback!

THE MYSTIC COVE SERIES

Wild Irish Heart

Wild Irish Eyes

Wild Irish Soul

Wild Irish Rebel

Wild Irish Roots: Margaret & Sean

Wild Irish Witch

Wild Irish Grace

Wild Irish Dreamer

Wild Irish Christmas (Novella)

Wild Irish Sage

Wild Irish Renegade

Wild Irish Moon

"I have read thousands of books and a fair percentage have been romances. Until I read Wild Irish Heart, I never had a book actually make me believe in love."- Amazon Review

A completed series.

Available in audio, e-book & paperback!

ALSO BY TRICIA O'MALLEY

STAND ALONE NOVELS

Ms. Bitch

"Ms. Bitch is sunshine in a book! An uplifting story of fighting your way through heartbreak and making your own version of happily-ever-after."

~Ann Charles, USA Today Bestselling Author

Starting Over Scottish

Grumpy. Meet Sunshine.

She's American. He's Scottish. She's looking for a fresh start. He's returning to rediscover his roots.

One Way Ticket

A funny and captivating beach read where booking a one-way ticket to paradise means starting over, letting go, and taking a chance on love…one more time

10 out of 10 - The BookLife Prize

ACKNOWLEDGMENTS

First, and foremost, my friends for their constant support, advice, and ideas. You've all proven to make a difference on my path. And, to my beta readers, I love you for all of your support and fascinating feedback!

And last, but never least, my two constant companions as I struggle through words on my computer each day - Briggs and Blue.

CONTACT ME

I hope my books have added a little magick into your life. If you have a moment to add some to my day, you can help by telling your friends and leaving a review. Word-of-mouth is the most powerful way to share my stories. Thank you.

Love books? What about fun giveaways? Nope? Okay, can I entice you with underwater photos and cute dogs? Let's stay friends, receive my emails and contact me by signing up at my website

www.triciaomalley.com

Or find me on Facebook and Instagram.
@triciaomalleyauthor

Made in United States
Orlando, FL
01 February 2024